Praise for Joseph L.S. Terrell's
Harrison Weaver Mysteries

Undertow of Vengeance, Joseph Terrell's fourth thriller in the Harrison Weaver crime writer series, and set in North Carolina's Outer Banks, is a knockout. With the deadpan savvy delivery of Humphrey Bogart as Sam Spade and the clipped declarative sentences of Dashiell Hammett, this volume, like its predecessors, reaches out in the very first sentence, grabs you by the lapels, and never lets up.
—Joseph Bathanti, former North Carolina Poet Laureate

Smooth writing from an eloquent storyteller goes down like fine scotch. *Undertow of Vengeance* is a keeper.
—Maggie Toussaint, Author, Cleopatra Jones Mysteries

"Every once in a while I'll pick up a book and from the first sentence, I'm engaged. Written with an extraordinary eye for detail yet in the sparse language of the journalist he once was, Terrell's novel is filled with wonderful dialogue, believable characters and just enough plot twists to keep the reader turning pages."
—Kip Tabb, Freelance Writer, former Ed. *North Beach Sun*

"Joe Terrell gets the Outer Banks just right, from crashing surf to the sordid crimes behind the tourism façade, to a thoughtful sleuth who can throw a punch and make a mean sweet tea."
—David Healey, Author, *The House That Went Down With The Ship*

"A smart, savvy combination of who-done-it and police procedural."
—Kathryn R. Wall, Author, the Bay Tanner Mysteries

Books by
Joseph L.S. Terrell

Harrison Weaver Mysteries

TIDE OF DARKNESS
OVERWASH OF EVIL
NOT OUR KIND OF KILLING
UNDERTOW OF VENGEANCE
DEAD RIGHT RETURNING
THE LAST BLUE NOON IN MAY
DEADLY DREAMS OF SUMMER

Mary Ann Little Weaver Mysteries

THE SERPENTINE FLOWER
A FLOWER SO FALLEN

Jonathan Clayton Novels
THE OTHER SIDE OF SILENCE
LEARNING TO SLOW DANCE

Stand Alones

A TIME OF MUSIC, A TIME OF MAGIC

A NEUROTIC'S GUIDE TO SANE LIVING

Deadly Dreams of Summer

A HARRISON WEAVER MYSTERY

JOSEPH L.S. TERRELL

BellaRosaBooks

DEADLY DREAMS OF SUMMER
ISBN 978-1-62268-149-5

First Printed: June 2019

Library of Congress Control Number: 2017943765

Also available as e-book: ISBN 978-1-62268-150-1

Printed in the United States of America on acid-free paper.

Cover design by Roo Harris.
Author and cover photographs by Lynne Scott Constantine.

Book design by Bella Rosa Books

BellaRosaBooks and logo are trademarks of Bella Rosa Books

10   9   8   7   6   5   4   3   2

This book is dedicated to my four blessings:
Michael, Emily, Jennifer, and Christopher.

Acknowledgments

First of all, thanks to those who helped with research on the evils of human trafficking: Michelle Wagner, a reporter who did a series on the subject for the *Outer Banks Sentinel*; Pam Strickland, founder of Eastern NC Stop Human Trafficking Now; Larry Likar, retired FBI special agent, for sharing his experience as an investigator into human trafficking; and to two investigators with the Department of Homeland Security, who for work purposes requested their names not be revealed, but who enlightened me considerably on how they do their job. For authoritative expertise on flying, I received considerable help from Phil Bowie, a talented author and expert pilot. He was most thorough and patient. A special thanks to first manuscript readers Veronica Moschetti Reich and to Cathy Kelly. Their insightful suggestions on editing and other matters in the story were most helpful. Then, a special hats off to Beth Terrell, a professional concept editor and excellent writer (using the byline Jaden Terrell) who worked tirelessly with me to make this story better. She's the greatest. Also, thanks to Roo Harris for his creative work on a cover design—again; and to Lynne Scott Constantine, the photographer who did the cover and the author photographs. And, finally, as always, I want to thank my editor and publisher, Rod Hunter of Bella Rosa Books, for his continuing faith in me.

—*JLST*

Author's Note:

This is a work of fiction, and while I have from time to time used the actual names of a few Outer Bankers, the main characters in this story are the figments of this writer's imagination and do not represent real people, living or dead. Most of the places mentioned in the story are real. As I have in the past, I've taken the liberty of compressing time to have the historic Dare County Courthouse as it was used in earlier times to house the sheriff's department as well as other county offices.

–JLST

Chapter One

You know how it is during the fading days of summer. One day tends to meld into the next, and you can't recall whether the rain was day before yesterday or three days ago. It's not that there's nothing to distinguish one day from the next, but you do get used to an evolving slower pace as the summer winds down. Certain routines become so common, even here on the Outer Banks, that a fuzziness envelopes your plans for the day and you begin to realize that in a few short weeks most of the tourists will be heading back to homes in Northern Virginia, Pennsylvania, Ohio, and elsewhere.

So one day begins to shuffle into the next like cards from a well-thumbed deck, a tad wilted from the summer's humidity.

But then suddenly one day slips out of that deck of cards.

And you realize, maybe not that day but soon, that nothing will ever be the same.

Your view of the human condition has changed.

Forever.

That day when things changed came on a Thursday, when Dee came to my little blue house in Kill Devil Hills. Dee's first name is something like Desdamonia, but I call her Dee because it's easier. She's from Honduras and has been here in the States for six years or more. Her English is almost understandable and she's been helping me with cleaning at my house off and on for three years. She does a good job and knows what to do without my telling her.

We have an agreement, though, when it comes to cleaning Janey's cage. Janey is my female parakeet, and she's pretty much a one-person bird. The first time Dee came to clean, she extended a finger through the bars in an offer of friendship that Janey rebuffed with a hard nip and a single, clearly enunciated word: "bitch." Female parakeets aren't supposed to mimic speech at all, but Janey knows two words—"bitch" and "shit." She says those two words perfectly, and says the first whenever Dee gets close to her cage.

Which is why cleaning the cage is my job.

When she arrives on cleaning day, Dee is usually very cheerful and comes in with a big smile. That Thursday morning, though, her smile seemed forced. She appeared subdued, distracted. She didn't hum that tune she usually does. She fumbled a bit in the kitchen, dropping a spoon and fork. After a while I asked her what was the matter. She came close to tearing up before answering.

I waited. She swallowed and then said, "My cousin, Marisa, she don't come home. Two days now."

"What do you mean? Not come home? Marisa doesn't live with you, does she, Dee?"

"No. Marisa live with those two other girls. They say she don't come home. She went to party. They don't know where. They call me. Want to know . . ." With difficulty, she swallowed again.

". . . if you've seen her?"

She nodded. "I tell them no. So they worry and I worry too."

I had met Marisa once or twice. A very good looking twenty-something brunette with a superb figure. Even at that first meeting, Marisa struck me as the type who might rather frequently find a young man who struck her fancy . . . and disappear for a day or more, until the passion cooled. She exuded sensuality and seemed to telegraph it. It was in the way she tilted her head and stood with one hip languidly thrust a bit to the side. A smile on her lips; eyelids taking on a sleepy bedroom cast.

"Oh, she'll show up in a day or so," I said. "Maybe she met . . . met a friend or something."

Dee wasn't buying that. She shook her head vigorously. "No, no. This is different. She invited to party that other girls in the house don't know and said she'd be back late that night." Dee put her palms together in a prayer-like fashion. She looked at me, apparently mulling over what I'd said about meeting a friend.

"Marisa talk big, but she not like . . . not like she act."

I nodded.

"So I worry she not come home." Dee bit down lightly on her lower lip, still staring at me. Dee usually worked very fast at cleaning my house. But she stood unmoving holding a dusting rag in one hand. "I think maybe you investigate?"

"Investigate? I'm not an investigator, Dee. I'm a writer. And besides I don't know what I would investigate."

"But you investigate and find crimes."

"We don't know there is any . . . any crime. She just hasn't shown up. A couple of days." I touched a hand to her shoulder. "Later, if you want to, you could go to the police."

"No police. Police, no, no." There was a flash of real terror in her eyes.

"Okay, no police." I guess I wanted to be of some comfort to her. "After you finish today, we'll go talk to the young women she lives with. Okay?"

She nodded, looked around as if she realized she was supposed to be cleaning. "Thank you," she said. Turning to the utility basket with her cleaning supplies, she pulled on a bright blue pair of rubber gloves, grabbed some spray cleaner and a brush, and headed to the bathroom.

My name is Harrison Weaver and I'm a writer, true crime mostly. I have actually investigated a number of crimes and written about them. So in that sense, I can understand why Dee thinks of me as an investigator.

No police. She was very adamant about that. I don't know whether that's a holdover from childhood experiences in Honduras, or worried about immigration here in the States. Maybe I should be concerned but I guess I've figured it best not to question her about her status. I'm personally glad she's here, and she's most welcome in my opinion. Let it lie.

After a while I went out on the deck and sat in the sun with a cup of coffee while she finished up. When I heard the vacuum running, that served as a signal she had about concluded. The vacuuming stopped and I heard her putting away the machine and gathering her cleaning supplies. I came inside, sliding the glass door to the deck behind me.

I paid her and said, "Want to go talk to Marisa's housemates?"

"Maybe you call?"

"Sure."

She scribbled down a number.

I called. After five rings a mechanical recording announced that the called party was not available.

She said, "They working somewhere." She compressed her lips again, and then bent over and busied herself picking up her utility basket.

"I'll try again later. Or tomorrow," I said.

As she started to leave, she faced me and said, "Maybe I worry too much."

But as it turned out, she was right to worry.

For what good it would have done.

Marisa's body washed up on the beach the very next morning.

Chapter Two

Shortly after eight Friday morning I got a call from my friend Duncan with the Dare County Emergency Service.

With no preliminaries he launched right in, but I could tell he was on his cell phone and talking privately so no one else could hear. In the background there was a subdued ruffled sound of the surf.

"A female body's on the beach. Washed up. Here on the south end of Coquina Beach." Duncan was my self-appointed "body spotter." Anytime he came upon a body or was called upon about a body—but not one involved in a fatal car accident or expired from apparent natural causes—he would phone me or get in touch with me in person. He operated under the false impression that I was interested in every cadaver as a possible crime story for one of the magazines I write for, or for even another book. Maybe a second made-for-TV movie. I didn't discourage him. You never can tell.

Probably because of my conversations yesterday with Dee, there was something about this news from Duncan that set off a warning spark of concern.

"What age woman?" I asked. "A beach-goer? Swimmer? Caught in a rip-tide?"

"Young," he said. "Probably twenties. Swimmer? Naw, I don't think so. She's fully clothed. No obvious trauma to her body."

"What color hair?"

"Black, or real dark brown. Black, I guess. She looks sort of Latino." He paused a moment. "But been in the water a day or more, I guess."

That feeling of concern grew stronger.

I heard more activity in the background.

"I gotta go," he said. "Dare County deputies just got here."

He signed off before I could thank him.

I swilled down the remainder of my now-lukewarm coffee, made a quick trip to the bathroom, washing and drying my hands more or less; pulled my cell phone from its charger and stuck it in my pocket; grabbed my car keys, spoke to my parakeet out of habit, and I was out the kitchen door and down the outside steps.

Backing my Subaru Outback from the carport, I turned it around in the cul-de-sac and drove fast up toward Highway 158, which we call the Bypass (even though it bypasses absolutely nothing; both sides of the five-lane road are lined with restaurants and businesses of all types). It runs north and south along this section of the Outer Banks. The Beach Road, or Highway 12, the only other north-south road in the area, runs more or less parallel to the Bypass.

Luckily, I was catching all of the lights on green as I headed south, making good time, and only bumping the speed up a tad over the 50 mph posted limit.

At Whalebone Junction, where the highway veers off to the right toward Roanoke Island and on beyond to the mainland, I swung to the left and picked up Highway 12 south toward Oregon Inlet. I checked my watch. I wanted to get there before they'd moved the body. With the Dare County deputies at the site, that could mean they were treating this as a suspicious death and things might be going at a more methodical pace.

I pushed the speed up a bit more, and more.

Shortly, Bodie Lighthouse came into view a good distance away on my right. Coquina Beach would be on the left, the ocean side.

I swung into the south parking area, getting as close to the right as I could. An unoccupied Dare County Sheriff Department sedan was parked almost at the walk-through across the dunes. Other four-wheel-drive vehicles would be down on the beach.

Wearing khaki shorts, a not-so-fresh T-shirt and ratty sockless sneakers, I tromped across the dunes cut-through into deep sand. I could see a Dare County sheriff's vehicle on the hard-packed sand not far from the surf. A beach rescue motorcycle type was pulled alongside a Dare EMT ambulance. Five or six people, most in uniforms, stood around in a loose semicircle.

Four beach goers stood solemnly near the surf's edge, several yards away from the officers and medical techs. They appeared to be talking quietly, very subdued. Young Deputy Dorsey stood sentinel to keep any curiosity seekers back a distance.

Dorsey nodded at me as I approached. Standing on the much firmer sand of the beach, I stopped to speak to him. He looked like he'd rather not be here. His reddish hair was cut short and his scalp was becoming more visible in the front. He wore cop sunglasses but I could still see his eyes and the fact that he squinted in the brightness of the day. I realized that as usual I had come out without sunglasses. Facing east, I squinted big time.

I inclined my head toward the group clustered near the ambulance. "Chief Deputy Odell Wright?"

"Yes, sir. He's there. You wanna see him?" With the slightest hint of a shrug, he said, "Go on over."

"Thanks," I said.

On the sand near, beyond the surf, a limp yellow tarp draped over the form of a body. I tried not to think about the possibility. The long shot that it might be. Yet, I couldn't shed that nagging feeling.

I moved toward the group. Duncan, wearing a blue shirt with the EMT emblem, glanced in my direction and then busied himself with the door handle of the ambulance as if he didn't know me.

Standing silently with his back toward me, Chief Deputy Odell Wright had his head downcast, his eyes on the covered lifeless form before him. His arms hung down by his side; he clenched and unclenched his left fist several times.

I approached him. He nodded. There was no trace of surprise at my being there. It was as if he'd gotten used to seeing me show up at scenes in the past. Maybe he figured I had a police scanner and monitored the calls—which I did not—or that someone tipped me off, as someone had. And, truth be known, maybe he didn't much care how I managed to show up: I just did.

Odell is a shade over six feet, a bit taller than me. His skin is coffee-colored, and his close-cropped dark hair now has a touch of silver at the temples. With an aquiline nose, his face in profile has always reminded me of an ancient Roman coin. While he has a wry sense of humor that I love, there was no humor in his countenance today.

Nor certainly none in mine.

Quietly I said to him, "Any identity?"

Odell shook his head. "Nothing. No ID at all. Right now, she's a Jane Doe." Then he turned his face toward me, seeming to take interest in me for the first time. "You think you might know her? That why you're here?" His lips formed a humorless half-smile. "I mean, another apparent drowning during the summer doesn't usually rouse your interest."

"A young woman I know is concerned about her cousin who's been missing a couple of days. That's all."

"A Latin cousin? Latino?"

I nodded. I didn't feel good about this.

He bent down, one knee almost touching the damp sand,

and took an edge of the tarp in his fingers. He trained his eyes up at me. "Take a look?"

I nodded again.

He lifted a corner of the tarp, exposing the face and dark matted hair.

No question about it.

The dulled, half-lidded eyes that stared back at me belonged to Marisa.

Chapter Three

Deputy Odell Wright kept his gaze on my face.

"I know her," I whispered.

He re-covered her face.

"Marisa," I said. "I don't know her last name. But I know who does." My voice was barely audible above the ceaseless groaning of the surf. Odell watched me as I talked and had no trouble knowing what I said. The tide was receding.

Odell placed one hand on his knee and hoisted himself up. "We'll take the body into Manteo." He mentioned the funeral home. He watched me again. "Your person can make a positive ID."

I nodded. I hated for Dee to have to do it, but it was necessary. "I'll bring her there," I said.

Odell was quiet. I became more conscious of the surf. Living here, you get almost used to the sound of the ocean. You don't hear it all the time, even when you stand near the great expanse of water. It becomes so much a part of all that is around you that you lose awareness—until something like this moment in time reminds you of that powerful force that faces you.

Then he spoke, as much to himself as to me: "It's puzzling though. What was she doing in the ocean? How did she get there?"

I tilted my head, gave him a questioning look.

He bent down and lifted the tarp off of Marisa's body.

I was startled. Duncan had said she was fully clothed, and she was indeed. She wore multicolored leggings, bright yellow, blue patterns intermingled, and a rather frilly dressy top that had shifted a bit off one shoulder. She had one canvas low-heel shoe on her left foot; her right foot was bare, her toenails painted a bright red.

She had been attired for a party.

It obviously hadn't ended well.

Odell saw the expression on my face. "Not exactly dressed for the beach, was she?"

Three more beach goers had joined the others. They craned their necks to see what was going on. Odell covered the body again. He spoke to one of the medical techs. "You can move her in a few minutes."

The medical tech, a husky female, did a short affirmative nod.

"Photos?" I said.

"Deputy Dorsey already shot some."

I stepped closer to Odell. "How the hell she get in the water? Fall off a boat? A pier?"

"That's what I've wondered," he said. He rubbed his chin; dropped his hand to his side again. That clenching and unclenching of his fist. He stared at me a moment before he spoke. "There was no call from the Coast Guard or anyone else about a person being overboard. No reports from the piers to rescue."

I said, "If she'd been at a party aboard a boat and fallen off, someone would have radioed Coast Guard, or rescue. A Mayday call to someone."

"Unless, maybe, no one noticed," he said, not sounding at all convinced at that thought.

Neither was I.

He stepped back from the body as Duncan and the other medic came over and stood with a folded stretcher. They waited for Odell to give the word. "Go ahead," he said, and then mentioned the funeral facility in Manteo where a positive identification would be made before the body was taken to Greenville for an autopsy. A procedure would determine whether drowning was actually the cause of death as it appeared and whether there were any extenuating circumstances, like maybe drugs.

As they gingerly moved Marisa's body on to the stretcher and then slid her into the rear of the ambulance, Odell and I stood there watching. We kept silent.

"She was supposed to be going to a party," I said. I couldn't remember whether I had already mumbled that to Odell.

He said. "We need to determine where that party was that she was going to."

"If her housemates even know," I said.

"And whether she got there," Odell added.

We watched the rescue vehicle move slowly across the sand to the cut-through between the dunes. Deputy Dorsey watched us, I assumed waiting for an all clear from Odell. Two of the male beach goers approached Dorsey. I heard him say "a drowning victim" and then something else that I couldn't catch.

I trudged beside Odell as he headed toward the dunes and the parking area beyond. His head inclined downward, apparently in thought. He stopped momentarily. "The so-called party might have been on a boat." Then he continued walking.

We got to the sheriff department sedan, my Outback right beside it. We hadn't spoken since his last statement. He leaned his back against the front fender on the driver's side, his head still tilted down in thought. "If she fell off the boat, why wasn't it reported?"

Then I said something I'd been mulling over in my mind. A mental leap, I know, but I said, "Maybe she jumped. Maybe she was trying to get away from the party."

He looked at me. He kept silent.

I continued. "Maybe the people giving the party didn't want it known she was there. That's why they didn't report it."

I could tell he weighed this thought, and I wasn't at all sure it wasn't something he had already played with in his mind.

He straightened up, put his hand on the handle of the sedan. "We've got to get with that person who knows the victim. We need a positive ID, last name, all of that."

"Want to follow me?" I asked.

"Sure."

I started to move away and get in my car, but I sensed he wanted to say something else. "Yes?" I said, turning back toward him.

"She wasn't the only one missing. We had separate reports late yesterday that two other young females are missing. At least, their friends think they're missing."

I stepped closer. I'm sure my face registered an "oh, shit" expression.

"They're both here for the summer as foreign workers. From Eastern Europe, or part of Russia. I've got it in my notes. Where they're from."

I stared at him. Odell returned my gaze.

"That's very strange," I said. Maybe it was part of my nature as a crime writer, but I had a tendency to start connecting dots—sometimes when there weren't obvious dots.

Softly he said, "What's strange is that these two young women were supposed to be going to a party, also."

Now it was time to say it aloud, not just think it: "Oh, shit," I said.

Chapter Four

We started to get into our vehicles, and I thought about Dee and her reaction when I mentioned going to the police. I turned back to Odell. He had one leg already in his cruiser.

"Instead of following me, maybe it'd be best if we met you at the funeral home," I said. "No sense in spooking her any more than I have to, with the two of us pulling up in front of her house."

He understood. "I'll meet you there in, say, thirty minutes. Forty-five?"

"I'll try to make it as close to thirty as possible."

"See you in about forty-five."

He followed me up Highway 12 until Whalebone Junction. He swung to the left; I kept straight toward Nags Head and Kill Devil Hills. The intersection where we parted got its name from the legend that years ago a local had recovered the jawbone of a large whale that he charged a tiny fee for people to see.

Traffic got heavier as I drove past Tanger outlets, then the mall, and pleasantly neat and colorful Outer Banks Hospital. People up and getting out on this beautiful sunny Friday toward the end of summer. Many cars from out-of-state. Tourists on their last hurrah.

Dee lives not far from me in Kill Devil Hills, west side of the Bypass toward the sound. Her husband, Julio, works for one of the local air conditioning businesses. They have a four-year-old son. If Dee doesn't have a cleaning job today —and she doesn't work every day—she'll be home with the little one. If she is working somewhere, the young babysitter will know where. I had decided not to call her in advance. Just show up.

I knew damn well she would be very, very emotional about what I would be asking her to do—come identify the body as that of her cousin.

Her Nissan van was in her driveway. That meant she was home. I cut the engine on my Subaru but sat there a few seconds before taking a deep breath—and probably a sigh— and got out and went up the side steps of her house, which like so many of the others was on stilts. Before I could knock, Dee came to the door, pushed the screen open and stood before me on the small porch. Her little son, his hair as black as coal, hung to her tights-clad leg. He studied me silently. Worry lines creased her forehead. She knew I wouldn't have shown up unless I had a serious message. Dread was in her eyes. But she breathed evenly, maintaining control, waiting for me to speak. My expression, I'm sure, telegraphed something to her.

"I hate to bring you this terrible news, Dee, but your cousin is deceased. She is dead. Drowned."

"Drowned? Drowned?" Tears welled in her eyes almost immediately. But her composure was steadier than I thought it would be. "But she could swim." She shook her head, as if erasing thoughts. "She going to a party. Not swimming."

"The ocean," I said. "The ocean is more dangerous than people think." I didn't want to say, not yet anyway, that Marisa was indeed dressed for a party—not for swimming.

She swallowed but held her head high, steeling herself. She squared her shoulders. I was amazed. I had thought she would practically collapse. Her words were even, and I could understand her accent completely: "Where is she?"

"She's at a funeral home in Manteo." I paused a moment

and licked my dry lips. "I've got to ask you to come with me to . . . to give a positive identification . . . and give other information. Her last name. How to get in touch with other relatives." I shuffled a bit on my feet as if trying to get comfortable. In a way, she was doing better than me.

She stared at me. Her eyes still glistened with tears. She wiped her right eye with the back of her hand. Head still high. "I don't want to do that, you know."

"But you've got to."

"I know," she said softly. "I know." She glanced around us as if it occurred to her that we were standing there on the small porch. "Come inside," she said, and turned and held the screen door open for me.

We stepped into the kitchen. It was sparse but very neat, as was the living room, which I could see beyond the kitchen. A few children's toys were on the living room floor and on a coffee table. That was the only clutter.

Her little boy stood to one side but kept staring up at his mother, then zeroing in on me, back to his mother.

Dee picked up her cell phone from the kitchen counter. "I call Julio. He come home." She punched in a number, waited a moment and then began to speak Spanish. Her voice choked once or twice, and the tears appeared again, but she maintained stoic composure. "Okay," she said in English. "Okay."

She ended the call and turned to me. "He comes home. Stay with Christopher." Her son heard his name and looked expectant. He knew something was up. Dee compressed her lips. "How she drowned?"

I still didn't want to go into too much detail. "Somehow or another she got in the ocean, or fell in, or something."

She gazed at me as if trying to determine if I was telling her all. Then she nodded.

Maybe it was experiences from back in Central America, but it appeared to me that death—sudden, unexpected death—was not such a foreign thing to her. The way she handled the news continued to surprise and impress me. I saw a different Dee than the shy young woman who came to my house to clean.

"Julio be here in a minutes," she said. She appeared to be mulling something over in her mind. Then she said, "I call the girls she live with. See if they can go with us to the funeral home."

"Yes," I said. "That would be good."

She got on her cell phone again, called one number. No answer. She called another number, waited a few seconds and then began to speak Spanish. I caught only a word or two. One of the words was *muerta* . . . dead. Dee listened for a moment or two, nodding, and making something of a consoling sound. I also heard the word *ahogada*, which I think meant drowned. Then Dee spoke steadily for a few more minutes and sounded as though she pleaded with the person on the other end of the call. She put the phone down.

Her chin up, she said, "Adelia go with us." She shrugged. "She don't want to go, but upset and not want to *not* go."

"I understand," I said.

A couple of minutes more and I heard a vehicle pull in the driveway. I glanced out the window. It was Julio in a company panel truck with the air conditioning logo on the side. He came up the stairs quickly, and little Christopher hurried to the door to greet him. Julio patted Christopher on the head but kept his eyes on Dee. He nodded at me and perfunctorily extended his hand for a quick greeting.

He is a bit darker than Dee and his features are more like those of the original inhabitants of Central America, not the European Spanish heritage that Dee possesses.

They spoke in Spanish. Then Dee said something else to him and turned to leave the kitchen, stopped, and spoke to me in English, that stoic expression on her face and in the way she stood. "We go in a minute. Pick up Adelia on the way." She went back toward their bedroom.

Julio shook his head sadly and extended his hand again as if we hadn't already greeted one another.

"Where was she found?" he said. His English was easier to understand than Dee's.

I told him she had washed up at the south end of Coquina Beach.

Julio frowned, processing that information.

"Officials don't know where she went in the ocean," I said. "Not yet, anyway."

Dee came out of the bedroom area. She had changed into a long, plain skirt and a dark colored top. Her hair, which undone hung down almost midway on her back, was pinned up in a lose bun. She looked pretty.

Little Christopher realized his mother was about to leave, and he began a tearful protest, but Julio picked him up and cradled him; that seemed to satisfy him.

"We'll be back as soon as possible," I said. "It shouldn't take long."

Julio leaned forward and gave Dee a light kiss on the lips and managed to work one hand free enough from Christopher to pat her on the shoulder. Christopher tried to reach out for his mother. Julio leaned back and Dee and I went out the kitchen door and down the steps to my car.

We drove out to the Bypass, turned north a short distance, and moved to the center lane to make a left turn onto West Durham Street. A block or so down the street Dee pointed to a small gray house. I pulled in the drive. An older model Toyota was parked far to the left, partly on the grassless yard. Dee tilted her head toward the car. "Marisa's," she said.

Dee started to get out but we saw Adelia coming out of the house toward us. Adelia carried a few extra pounds. Like Dee and the late Marisa, she was in her twenties, maybe late twenties. She was not as pretty as Dee. She wore patterned leggings and a flowered top, hanging loose.

I got out and opened the back door for her.

She tried a smile that didn't quite work and mumbled, "*Gracias.*"

Then she and Dee began to converse rapidly to each other in Spanish, and I backed up, drove to the Bypass, turned south and headed toward Manteo.

And the funeral home.

Chapter Five

At the funeral home, I pulled around to the tree-shaded left side and nosed into a space. The parking area was virtually empty; however, a Dare County Sheriff's Department cruiser was out front. Had to be Chief Deputy Odell Wright. I noticed that Dee eyed the cruiser as we went by it. Her only visible sign of nervousness was the way she clasped her hands tightly in her lap. She kept her lips compressed. I glanced in the rearview mirror at Adelia, who sat straight but had seemed to shrink, miniaturizing herself. Like a disappearing act.

The three of us got out of the car and approached the front door of the funeral home. The door gleamed white, with a dark trim along the frame. Welcoming design to the door, yet subdued enough to make one realize it was a serious place you were about to enter.

I entered first, Dee right behind me, and Adelia bringing up the rear, her eyes skittering about as if she might flee at any moment.

Inside, I was assailed by that almost overwhelming floral scent. I expected to hear soft music, but it was silent. Immediately a serious young man, neatly attired in a tieless dress shirt and suit jacket, came from an adjoining room.

He held out his hand and smiled sympathetically, and shook hands with each of us in turn.

Odell sat quietly over to one side in a straight-back upholstered chair. He rose when we came in.

Dee saw him. I felt her stiffen beside me.

Odell nodded at me and then said, *"Como esta?"* to Dee.

She mumbled a response in Spanish to his greeting. She appeared to relax a bit after he said something else to her in Spanish.

I spoke to Dee. "He is my friend, my *amigo.*"

She managed a smile of sorts.

He spoke again in halting Spanish. I understood a word that sounded like condolences.

She nodded, acknowledging his words.

Then the young man asked if we wanted to view the deceased.

"Only enough to verify the identification," I said.

Adelia said something to Dee and pointed to the chair that Odell had been sitting in.

To me, Dee said, "Adelia want to stay here."

"I understand." Then, concentrating my eyes on Dee, I said, "You okay?"

Lips compressed, she bobbed her head in a quick affirmative. Odell stood beside us. She seemed more relaxed with him now, mostly I assume, because he spoke a little Spanish, and the fact that I had said he was my friend, and perhaps, too, because his skin was a little darker than hers.

Adelia shrunk herself into the straight-back chair.

The young man opened a door for us at the end of the foyer and we followed him back through another door into a smaller room with two formal straight back upholster chairs against the wall. It was quiet. I could hear Dee breathing beside me.

There before us was a draped table—not a coffin but not one of the shiny silver tables I'd seen before in a morgue—and a sheet-covered body.

The young man stood silently near the head of the table, one hand lightly holding an edge of the sheet. He looked at each of us in turn.

He saw the slight movement of my head, and he eased the sheet back to uncover Marisa's face. They had not done any cosmetic work on her, but her hair was neater than it had been at the beach. She didn't appear quite as bad as I was afraid she would. Maybe they *had* done a little something to her face. Her eyes were closed gently.

Dee sucked in her breath, stiffened, and grabbed tightly to my upper arm. It was obvious, as I knew it would be.

Dee stared at her cousin a few more seconds, then turned her head away. Tears welled in her eyes.

Very quietly, Odell asked, "Is this your cousin? You are positive?"

"*Si*," Dee said. "*Esta es Marisa.*"

The young man covered Marisa's face.

"Thank you," I whispered, and we turned and went back to the foyer. Adelia rose from the chair when we came in silently. She looked at Dee, and Dee nodded.

"Would you like to sit down?" Odell said to Dee, indicating the chair Adelia had vacated.

Without speaking, Dee went to the chair and sat. Odell stood beside her. As much to me as to Dee, he said, "I know you don't feel like it, but I do need her full name and any addresses or relatives you can give me."

Barely audibly, Dee said, "Okay."

Adelia said something to Dee in softly spoken Spanish. Dee shook her head and gave Adelia a dismissive little flick of one hand.

To me, Adelia said, "Go outside now?"

I looked questioningly at Odell and Dee. He said, "Fine. We'll be a minute or two." He had taken a small notebook from one pocket, a pen poised as he stood near Dee.

Adelia and I went outside. I breathed deeply. The air was better. Even with a whiff now and then of the exhaust of a passing car, it was better outside. Not that heavy floral.

We stood near my Outback. I leaned against a front fender. "Want to sit inside?" I asked. I moved back and opened the rear door on the passenger side.

"Maybe yes," she said, and slid into the seat and once again appeared to make herself smaller.

I stared off across Budleigh Street and then at the sky. The sun had moved west, the humidity was down, and it was a lovely afternoon. Except for what nagged at me. How did Marisa get in the ocean?

Twisting a bit toward Adelia, I tried to sound casual. "Where was the party Marisa was going to?"

She shook her head. "We don't know. She was happy to go. She did say it would start one place and then go other place."

"You don't know either of the places?"

She shook her head. "No."

In less than five minutes, the front door of the funeral home opened and Dee came out with Odell right behind her. He walked with her over to my car. I opened the front passenger door. Odell was thanking her and said he would be in touch.

I couldn't read anything from Odell's face.

When Dee got in the car, I closed her door. Odell stood there a moment. To me he said, "I'm going to call your friend Agent Twiddy, chat with him a bit." He straightened his shoulders. "You can call me tomorrow."

I knew the significance of calling Agent Twiddy—that's SBI Agent T. (for Thomas) Ballsford Twiddy, known to me and his friends simply as "Balls."

Odell thought, the same as I did, that there was some-thing very peculiar, something suspicious, about Marisa's death.

A person, fully clothed in a dressy outfit, doesn't simply show up drowned on one of our beaches without anyone reporting it.

It didn't make sense.

I learned a long time ago as a reporter and crime writer that if something doesn't make sense, then something is afoul.

Chapter Six

We drove from the funeral home in Manteo toward the beach and Kill Devil Hills. None of us spoke. The sun was behind us as we approached Pirate's Cove. The dozens of large boats gleamed in the sun. Many of the boats were charter fishing boats that would leave the Pirate's Cove marina, head out into the sound and then south toward Oregon Inlet and the ocean. We started up the high bridge over Roanoke Sound and I thought about how some of the boats could be used for partying, with maybe a little fishing thrown in, or maybe not.

From the top of the bridge, we could glimpse the Wanchese peninsula off to the right; the huge sand dune of Jockey's Ridge was on our left, barely visible. Depending on prevailing winds, Jockey's Ridge tended to grow and shrink during the seasons. No matter what the wind, it was the highest sand dune on the East Coast. Some authorities say the dune moves southward about an inch each year. Maybe it does.

As we started down the bridge, Adelia said something in Spanish to Dee, who sat there staring straight ahead. Dee appeared to come alert, and she responded to Adelia. I didn't know what they were saying, but I gathered enough to sense that Adelia asked Dee how it went with Deputy Wright.

Dee looked at me. "Funeral?" she said.

"I don't know. We'll figure it out." I had wondered about that earlier, and whether Dee and the family had funds for it; whether Marisa would be cremated, how it would be handled. "Will you get in touch with Marisa's mother and father? Other relatives?"

Dee said, "*Si.*"

I nodded.

We drove up to West Durham Street to let Adelia off, and then I went back to Dee's, parked in her driveway. "You've been very brave, Dee."

"Thank you," she said. Then, with a weak smile, she said, "*Muchas gracias.*"

"*De Nada,*" I said.

She opened the door and got out. She waved a hand at Julio and her son who had stepped out on the porch. She walked toward her house as if she were very, very tired. I drove away.

When I got back to my house, Janey chirped as I came in. I spoke to her and leaned in toward her cage and said, "Hello, Janey." She did her little head-bobbing dance as a further way of greeting.

I propped my elbows on the kitchen counter and realized how tired I was. Bone weary. Fatigued, too, from not eating. Hell, that just occurred to me. I got a glass of orange juice and drank it down. That should help some.

I glanced at my watch. I wanted to call Elly. Almost quitting time for her. Maybe I could catch her at work, or certainly at home. Friday afternoon. I'd like to see her tonight.

Elly Pedersen is my sweetheart, and has been for more than two years now. Her first name is really Ellen, but virtually everyone calls her Elly. Once in a while her mother calls her Ellen. That's when she wants to make a special point. I met Elly shortly after I moved to these barrier islands off the coast of North Carolina, the Outer Banks.

Elly has a son, Martin, who is five now, and has come to the point that he speaks to me quite willingly. He treated me with grave suspicion for a year or more. Like me, Elly lost her spouse almost four years ago. Her husband was a classical musician, cello, and his health had always been rather delicate. He died after a short but virulent type of flu. That was when Elly and infant Martin moved from Raleigh back to the Outer Banks, where she had grown up. She still has some of that fast-disappearing native "hoigh toide" accent that I love.

I went over to the corner of the living room to my landline phone. For once I didn't have to step over the neck of my bass fiddle. I'd actually put it upright in its stand after practicing a bit yesterday and before Dee came to clean. I punched in Elly's work number at the Register of Deeds office.

She answered on the first ring, and I told her I didn't know whether I would catch her or not.

"We were closing up," she said, "and I've wondered where you've been all day and what you're up to." A hint of a chuckle. "Probably getting into some kind of trouble."

"Well, maybe," I said.

She immediately caught the gravity in my voice. "I was teasing," she said, "but you're not. Something's up."

On Thursday night, in a telephone conversation with Elly, I had mentioned that Dee was concerned about her cousin. So now I was to tell her what had happened today. I went into quite a bit of detail. I heard one of her coworkers tell her goodnight and have a nice weekend, and I kept talking and she kept listening. Every now and then she would say something like, "Oh, my goodness. That's awful."

Then I told her what Odell had said about the two other young women reported missing.

Elly said, "I heard something about that today from Mabel." Mabel had worked in the sheriff's office for decades; she knew everything about everything that was happening, and she talked with Elly frequently.

"What do you think?" Elly said.

"I don't know. But Odell is going to call Balls, Agent Twiddy. Run it by him."

"Something bad going on?" There was concern in her tone.

"I don't know. Maybe."

We were silent for a moment or two. "Time for you to go home," I said.

"Yes. Yes, it is." Her voice was hesitant. Then she forced a more cheerful, "Tonight? Why don't you come eat with us?" She and Martin lived with her mother in a neat little Sears & Roebuck house of the 1930s on the west side of Manteo, near the airport.

I realized I still hadn't eaten. "Well, that does sound nice, but . . ."

"No problem, I'm sure," she said. "Mother still has some of that ham left."

"Does sound good. But check with her first."

"See you about six?"

"Thank you, Elly. You are sweet."

"Got to keep you fed," she said. Then she added, "Because I know if Agent Twiddy's going to be around you'll be hanging out with him and sticking your nose into whatever is going on."

"See you at six," I said with a laugh. Over the period we had been together, Elly has gotten to know me real well. At first she had trouble accepting the fact that I'm a crime writer and that I have a penchant for getting involved in investigations. And more than once, this tendency of mine has put me in real danger—even wounded once—and put her in real danger too, and pain, shortly after I moved here and met her. But she's mostly overcome the psychological trauma of that incident. Still, I know she struggles with it and if she didn't care for me as much as she does, I know it would be even more difficult for her.

I took a long hot shower and that made me feel better. Dressed in shorts, golf shirt and boat shoes. Typical attire for late summer at the Outer Banks. Formal enough, too.

Making sure Janey had fresh water and a treat of a millet sprig, I prepared to leave for Elly's. To Janey I said, "Clean that cage tomorrow. Promise." I latched the sliding door to the deck, checked the lights—leaving one lamp on because I don't like coming back to a darkened house. Glanced around and started for the kitchen door and the outside steps.

And the phone rang.

Backtracked across the living room and answered the phone.

It was Balls, and as usual, he started right in. "Listen," he said, "if I've gotta spend part of my Saturday coming down to the Outer Banks to see Odell, you're gonna have to buy me breakfast at Henry's. Three-egg omelet with extra toast and jelly, tall glass of tomato juice with crushed ice."

"There's plenty of jelly right there on the table," I said. "You don't have to order extra jelly."

"No coffee," he said. "I'm cutting back."

"When have you ever cut back on anything?" I said.

"The new me," he said.

"Yeah, right."

Balls lived with his wife Loraine in Elizabeth City, forty-some miles from the Outer Banks. I'd known Balls since my days as a reporter covering the police beat and politics. I had once helped him—quite unexpectedly—in uncovering a clue that led to his solving a really puzzling investigation into a homicide. Since that time, he's called me his Lucky Charm. Over the years he's come to trust me enough to allow me to tag along with him (on the sidelines) of a few of the things he might be investigating . . . or that I have become involved in. He knows I will not write anything prematurely, and he knows I will keep my mouth shut, from time to time.

He's a big tough guy, built somewhat like a burlap bag filled with wet sand, and I do believe that a punch into his midsection would result in nothing more than a bruised fist.

For some time he's sported a Tom Selleck type moustache, so he looks rather dashing, in a burly sort of way.

To top it off, he's one hell of an investigator.

Naturally, I agreed quite readily to breakfast Saturday at Henry's, just up the Bypass from my house.

But right now, I scurried to get on my way to see sweet Elly.

Chapter Seven

Heading south on the Bypass, the traffic was heavy. After all, it was a Friday night, start of the weekend, still tourist season, and lots of folks were getting off work or looking for places to eat dinner. Many of the drivers, too, were not sure where they wanted to go. Just something you contend with. But after many years in the DC area, this didn't seem all that difficult to me.

Traffic got lighter as I passed beyond French Fry Alley, a locals' moniker for a spate of fast-food places clustered along the Bypass. Then beyond the YMCA, a short distance beyond Mile Post 11, my speed picked up to a tad over the posted 50 mph.

At Whalebone Junction I swung left and headed toward Little Bridge and then the high-rise Washington Baum Bridge over Roanoke Sound. The bridge is a mile long and rises eighty feet above the water at its apex. Love the view from the top. Ahead of me in the late afternoon sun, the trees off in the west become silhouetted in black, and the marsh grass or whatever it is that grows in the wetland beyond Pirate's Cove always reminds me of the pelt of a huge animal that lies there basking in the sun or twilight, waiting to pounce.

I drove through Manteo and past the "new" Christmas Shop—former owner and founder of the Christmas Shop

Edward Greene has officially retired and the present owners have taken it over—and on westward on Highway 64 toward the airport and Fort Raleigh. After a left turn and then another one, I pulled into Elly's mostly gravel driveway and past the huge live oak tree with its drooping branches that make a tent-like playground for Martin and his little next-door friend Lauren. The ground under the live oak has been worn grassless and two toy trucks and maybe the piece of a doll lie near the big trunk of the tree.

When I stopped the car, Elly appeared on the porch, Martin standing beside her. She waggled the fingers of one hand and smiled. She had changed from her office attire and looked great in a trim pair of tan shorts, a loose fitting collared cotton top and flip-flops. Nice, long legs.

Over the years, the house has been added to: the kitchen expanded toward the rear, an upstairs finished, and the living room extended off to the right. A porch with wide plank boards runs across most of the front. Three steps lead up to the porch. The land on which the house is built, and others in the general area, is far enough from the water that flooding is not a problem. No houses on stilts, like mine.

I came up on the porch, took Elly's hand and pecked a discreet kiss on the cheek. Martin eyed me and I spoke to him and he nodded solemnly.

Inside, the living room always looks so comfortable and lived in. As usual, the crossword section of *The Virginian-Pilot* was folded atop one of the sofa's end tables. From a quick glance, the puzzle appeared to have been completed. Elly's good at them. And the Lawler book I had lent her, *The Secret Token,* about efforts to establish a permanent English colony on Roanoke Island, had a bookmark in it and lay on the coffee table. That group of more than a hundred men, women, and children—including Virginia Dare, the first child of English heritage born on these shores—disappeared and became known as *The Lost Colony.*

I could smell the meal being prepared, and I realized

anew how hungry I was.

Mrs. Pedersen came out from the kitchen, smiled a hello, and said, "Supper will be ready in a minute or two." She's a bit taller than Elly, ramrod straight, with short iron gray hair that she brushes back severely. Elly obviously took after her late father's build, coloring, and somewhat delicate features. A Coast Guardsman from Minnesota, he met Elly's mother when stationed in the area. He was lost at sea when Elly was still a child.

Without comment, Martin showed me a drawing he had done of a tree and a sunny sky. "That's really good, Martin. You're getting better all the time."

He nodded agreement.

In a quiet voice to me, Elly said, "As I was leaving the courthouse today, I spoke again to Mabel. Or rather she spoke to me. About that incident that you saw today, and the fact that Agent Twiddy is coming here tomorrow."

"Yes?" She had my full attention.

Mrs. Pedersen called from the dining room. "Supper's ready."

"I'll tell you later."

I was very much interested in hearing more.

We went into the dining room through a passageway that had originally probably been a doorway. The rather large wooden table, maybe even an antique, was covered with a white tablecloth and glasses with iced tea—sweetened—were at places for the three adults. Martin had some sort of juice.

"Looks awfully nice, Mrs. Pedersen," I said. "And smells good too."

She put a dish with hot biscuits on the table. Their aroma made my mouth water. I noticed, too, a dish of local honey and fresh butter. I could hardly wait. She served the ham steak on a platter with some type of floral design along the plate's edges that reminded me one my grandmother had years ago. Martin got a dish of macaroni and cheese and we got stewed fresh corn and sliced tomatoes, large ones that probably came from plants Mrs. Pedersen had in the backyard.

"I'm very lucky, Mrs. Pedersen. Thank you so much."

"Sit down and enjoy," she said.

I sat opposite Elly, who sat close to Martin, with Mrs. Pedersen to my right, closest to the kitchen. The meal was excellent, as I knew it would be.

Afterward, Mrs. Pedersen said, "What about dessert? There's some of that apple pie left."

I reached for another of her homemade biscuits. "If you don't mind, my dessert is going to be another one of your biscuits with whipped butter and honey."

"I love that, too," Elly said.

I started to say something about how they stay so trim with all this good food. But it's obvious their genes play a big part because Elly, I know, can eat anything she wants and plenty of it.

After supper, Elly and I went out to the chain-supported swinging bench on the front porch and sat side-by-side in the gathering dusk. A light breeze played gentle games with a lock of hair near her forehead.

"I know," she said, "you want to hear what Mabel said to me." She did a tiny laugh. "I'm surprised you were able to contain yourself during supper."

I tried a shrug. She knew it was a phony shrug. "Okay," I said. "Yes, please."

"She had already told me about, you know, the girl who drowned. The one you . . ."

"Yes, I know."

"But she said Odell and the sheriff were talking about that and also about the two girls who are missing. Mabel said the sheriff doesn't want to admit it, but he's afraid Odell is right."

I looked at her. She could see the questioning expression on my face, I'm sure.

Elly took a breath. "Well, Odell thinks that somehow the two things—the missing two and this young woman today—are connected. That something, maybe organized, is going on."

I was silent a moment or two. "Maybe that's one of the reasons Balls—Agent Twiddy—is coming down tomorrow."

With a sense of dismay, I shook my head. "Something organized . . . that's not good."

Chapter Eight

True to form, the next morning as breakfast time approached, Balls called on his cell phone to tell me he would swing by my house in five minutes and that he was hungry.

I was showered and dressed and ready for him. Decided to spend a minute or two on the bass fiddle. Tuning up with harmonics, using the bow, I was bringing the A-string up a fraction when I heard the rumble of his classic Thunderbird pulling into my cul-de-sac; then turning his car around, nose out as always. The car was his pride and joy, and I guess considered an antique now.

I laid the bass down on its side, quickly loosened the bow's tension a bit, spoke to Janey and headed for the door.

Balls hadn't cut the engine. It made a throaty, healthy sound. Not loud, but foretelling of power if needed. I opened the passenger door and squeezed in, being careful of his dashboard-mounted computer, radio, and other crap he had crammed in the front.

"I thought you might be still asleep," he said, giving me that sidelong grin of his.

Hooked my seatbelt. "Three-egg omelet, huh?" I said.

"Yeah, and you're paying."

I shrugged. "So what else is new?"

We pulled out to the Bypass and headed north a short distance to Henry's. As usual, the lot was crowded with the breakfast crowd. But Balls found a wide spot near the rear and backed into it perfectly, leaving plenty of room between his car and any who might park nearby.

"Why didn't we just walk from my house?" I said. "Parking here on the South Forty."

"Little bit of walking is good for you," Balls said, as we got out. I knew his sidearm—a mean-looking .45 caliber Glock was stored out of sight under the front seat. He locked the car, and tested the door out of habit to make sure.

Pretty Linda, the co-owner with husband Henry, was at the register. Good to see her. We spoke and then a hostess took us back to a booth on the left, and put two menus down on the table.

We sat with Balls facing me so he could keep an eye toward the front. Again, something out of habit. Little things I expected of him. "Can't help but flirt with the ladies, can you?" he said.

"Linda? She's a friend. Just speaking to her."

"Yeah." Then he added, "She is good looking."

A waitress I had seen before but whose name I couldn't remember, came up quickly with order pad in hand. We didn't really need the menus. Balls rattled off what he wanted, including the extra order of white toast and a large glass of tomato juice with crushed ice. I ordered an omelet also, but not with as many extra ingredients as Balls had. Ham and cheese only for me.

"You want extra toast also?" she asked.

"No thanks. But make it whole-wheat."

In very short order, our food came and we busily dug in. A pleasure watching Balls go after his food. The wire container with jelly packets was not safe from his attack. That extra toast was disappearing fast, along with the jelly. Empty jelly packets began to stack up beside his plate.

"Okay, Balls," I said, as I took a pause from eating. "I know you wanted to come down for breakfast, but that's not the real reason. What about Odell? What is it he wants to talk with you about?"

Balls crunched on the ice in his tomato juice before he answered. "None of your damn business." Then he grinned. "Well, actually there is something he's been working on that is none of your business. But the other thing, you know what it is. That drowning yesterday. He figures it as a suspicious death." He set the tall tomato juice down, glanced at me. "He figures that's probably the tip of the iceberg."

"What iceberg?" I said.

He forked in another mouthful of omelet. Getting close to the end of the three-egg monster. "Maybe human trafficking. Just maybe." Balls swallowed and then leaned forward. "The other two women reported missing. Supposed to be going to a party. Don't come back. The woman who drowned. Supposed to be going to a party also, ends up in the ocean."

I tried to act incredulous, a ploy to draw out more. "Aw, come on, Balls. That drowning was certainly puzzling. I mean, how did she get in the ocean? And how come no one reported it? She wasn't dressed for the beach. But to connect dots from that to . . . to something organized like . . . well, like human trafficking. I don't get it." I glanced around to make sure my comments were private. "But to make that link?" Then I gave it a bit more thought. "I know Odell, though, and I know he doesn't go off, say, half-cocked on theories."

I stared at Balls' face. His eyes were locked on me. I said, "Human trafficking? Here? At the Outer Banks?"

"Going on everywhere," he said. "Statistics say North Carolina ranks about eighth in the nation. Outer Banks is ripe for it. Perfect place for that kind of crap." His jaw muscles tightened, his lips in a hard line. "That kind of . . . of cruelty." He shook his head. "Mean," he said, "I'm talking really mean. Shit, evil."

I knew why the Outer Banks was especially susceptible. But I knew, also, that Balls wasn't through talking.

"Yeah," he said, "here at the Outer Banks you got a lot of young people coming down here for a big time. Maybe think they'll get good jobs for the summer. They work a bit at different jobs and have some fun. Then they give out a money, get more or less homeless. They're then easy picking for a trafficker."

The waitress came up and asked if we needed anything else. Even Balls said, "No thanks. It was good."

She put the check down between us, and I picked it up.

"Then, too," Balls said, still leaning toward me, "we've got these foreign kids that come here for the summer. That program that brings lot of 'em in from Eastern Europe, Russia, other places. Work at Food Lion, some of the restaurants. Some of them would like to stay. Uh-huh? In steps a trafficker, going to make it possible for them to live out their dream." He shook his head, anger beginning to build. "Oh, hell yeah. Live out their dream."

More anger built in Balls as he talked.

"And then they never get away, or if they do, they're traumatized for the rest of their lives." He shook his head again. "Or they end up in the drink like that young woman did yesterday."

We got up, I left a tip, and paid at the register. Spoke to Linda again. I tried a nice smile.

"Was everything all right?" A bit of concern in her voice.

"Oh, great," I said, "as always." I did more of a smile.

She nodded. Smiled in return, but not quite convinced.

I followed Balls outside to his Thunderbird in the South Forty.

He didn't speak. His head down. He muttered something that sounded like, "We'll get the sons a bitches."

We were silent most of the way toward Manteo and the courthouse. There had to be more to this so-called iceberg than I was privy to at the moment. I figured I'd keep my mouth shut, find out more about why Odell, and now obviously Balls, thought human trafficking was involved. Quite a leap between this one drowning, two young women missing, and human trafficking, but I knew what good investigators both of them were. Reserve judgment. As a wise editor told me once, "Do more reporting. Get more facts. Then the story will write itself."

So I sat back in the Thunderbird and watched the scenery. We passed the Christmas Shop and Darrell's Restaurant. Caught one of the lights on green, stopped at the next one; another block we made a right turn onto Budleigh Street.

Balls parked in a reserved spot at the courthouse. I didn't question his choice. We got out and I looked up at the old red bricks. The courthouse was built in 1904, a year after the Wright Brothers' historic flight up at what is now Kill Devil Hills. There's talk of constructing a much-needed county office complex on the eastern edge of town. Frankly, I love the old courthouse, but I'll admit it's getting a bit cramped, and some of the offices have had to take auxiliary quarters around town. Tacked on at the second story rear of the courthouse are a couple of jail cells, straight out of TV's fictional Mayberry. You'd almost expect to see Andy Griffith and Don Knotts at any moment.

Just as we stepped out on the sidewalk, a deputy opened the side door. He nodded a greeting to Balls and held the door open for him. We went inside and trudged up the back steps to the second floor.

"Too bad we're going up the back instead of the front so you could see your sweetie," Balls said. Elly's office in the Register of Deeds was inside on the left off the low front porch of the courthouse.

"It's Saturday, Balls."

"Oh, yeah. Days sort a running together."

It was quiet upstairs. The light was off in Sheriff Albright's office, although knowing him, he would probably drop by the office at some point today.

Chief Deputy Odell Wright stood tall in the hallway, watching us approach. We shook hands, and he tilted his head toward a room off to the right. "Sit in here?" he said. The room was used from time to time for interrogations. It contained a metal table with two chairs on each side. Odell went to the far side and Balls and I sat opposite him.

"Appreciate you coming down on a Saturday," Odell said to Balls.

Balls sucked on a tooth a moment. Then he said, "You've got this suspicious death, and you're thinking human trafficking. The two connected? Fill me in on your thought process. How're you connecting the dots?"

I sat quietly, like trying to be invisible so they would ignore me and keep on talking. I figured Balls may have asked Odell to "connect the dots" even though he knew what Odell would say, as if he hadn't himself already connected the dots. Maybe for my benefit?

Before answering Balls, Odell sat staring at his hands, extended on the table, fingers interlaced. His nails were neatly trimmed, and his fingers were long and tapered. His hands were those that might belong to a pianist or a violin player. Yet, I'd seen once how powerful those hands could be when he subdued a big guy who didn't want to be arrested.

Then Odell looked at Balls and spoke. "When this young woman showed up on the beach, apparently drowned —we'll get a final autopsy sometime Monday from Dr. Mordecai—and nobody reported her falling in the ocean or anything else, well that bothered me. Somebody would report it. But until then, I figured those two European young women had just taken off. Got tired of being here. Found boyfriends or something and they just wanted to disappear."

Balls was quiet, eyes on Odell and listening intently. As I was too.

"But late yesterday, I went up to Duck where those two women live. Met with their two roommates, the ones who'd reported the two missing." He shook his head. "Talk about human trafficking. As far as I'm concerned, it's going on quite legally. But it's not right."

Balls raised his eyebrows. "Yeah?"

"The four of them work for . . ." and he named a businessman I'd heard of before but didn't know personally. "He promised them each three hundred dollars a week." Odell did a wry curl of his upper lip. "Sounds good, doesn't it? Only problem is he charges them two hundred dollars a week for lodging. Four of them in the one large room, two bunk beds. So after their room rent, they get a hundred bucks a week, less taxes."

"Yeah," Balls said. "That's slave labor he's got there." He made a face. "Man, that ain't right."

"When I found that out, I figured at first that the two had just gotten tired of being taken, and took off." He paused, choosing his words. "But when I met with the two roommates and went to their room, I knew right away that wasn't the case. All of the female stuff belonging to the two women —their makeup and that sort of thing—was all in the bathroom or on the dresser. And their clothes, too, spread around. Nothing packed up."

Balls nodded very slowly, listening.

"Those two got dressed up that afternoon to go to a party —like this drowned woman got dressed up to go to a party."

Odell sighed. "Problem is, we don't have any idea where this party was, who was having it, or whether the two women and this drowning victim were all three going to the same party."

"Seems unlikely," Balls said. "But who knows? Any indication the three knew each other?"

"Not that I've been able to determine," Odell said. "But maybe all three knew the person or persons having the party."

I shifted in my seat. The chair was hard and uncomfortable, but truth be told I was probably squirming around
wanting to speak.

Balls cut his eyes over at me. "Yeah?"

I said, "Marisa's car was still in the driveway when I
took Dee around to get the roommate." I glanced from Balls
to Odell and back again. "Somebody had to pick her up to go
to that party she was supposed to be attending."

I turned to Odell. "I don't know whether the other two
women had a car or access to one."

"They didn't," Odell said.

"So somebody picked them up, too. Maybe neighbors
saw whoever picked them up to take them to this party." I
took a breath, wanting to get out thoughts before what I
considered my limited time to speak ran out. "As for parties,
we've almost got to assume that Marisa was going to a party
aboard a boat. Seems logical since she ends up in the ocean.
Maybe someone at one of the marinas saw a party boat going
out."

Odell nodded. "We'll be canvassing the neighborhoods
of both houses this afternoon." He ran a palm over his close-
cropped hair. "As for checking with marinas, we'll do that
of course, but there are so many boats coming and going
that . . ."

"Yeah," Balls said. "Good luck on the marinas."

I may have given the slightest shrug. I'd had my say,
just about. But I felt compelled to throw out some other
thoughts. "Maybe we got a serial killer. Not something
organized like trafficking. And maybe there's no connection
at all with these young women."

Balls was quiet for a moment, and so was Odell. Then
Balls said, "Yeah, we've tossed around other possibilities.
But still think we gotta settle best we can on one."

Then he was quiet, and so was Odell.

The devil's advocate approach I'd thrown out fell flat.
It's quite likely they knew something I didn't. At least that's

what I assumed.

In the silence that followed, I heard a low conversation out in the hall. Probably two deputies chatting. I couldn't understand what they were saying. I glanced at the round clock on the wall to the left. The second hand did little spasmodic jerks of passing time. Odell waited, glancing at Balls.

Finally Balls said, "Depending on what we find out about these two young women—the missing ones—we may have to call in the Feds, alert them. If we think it's kidnapping. Then it's a federal case."

"I'd rather we handled it ourselves," Odell said. "With your help, of course. The SBI. State, not the Feds if possible. I know they're good and all, but they have a tendency to want to take over."

Balls said, "Understand. But I know a Fed guy easy to work with. A good guy.

Odell said, "They may turn up. The women, I mean . . . not the FBI." He permitted himself a soft grin that faded quickly.

I couldn't help it. I said, "Yes, maybe turn up as dead bodies."

Odell had a sad expression around his eyes. He shook his head. "Hope not . . . but they should have turned up before now."

Balls sighed loudly and rose from his chair, pressed the small of his back with both hands. "Okay, enough of this. Let's get to work, Odell." He tilted his head toward me. "I'll run this dirty-neck newspaper guy back to his house. You follow me and then let's go talk to some of those neighbors. Somebody's got to have seen something."

Odell and I stood. Balls grinned at me. "You can stay home and practice your cello."

"It's a bass fiddle, Balls."

"Whatever."

He knew damn well I play bass and not cello, but it's sort of a running gag with him, goading me on when he can.

Truth be told, however, I wasn't planning to stay home. I was going to go over to see if Dee could help me out on where Marisa had worked. She cleaned houses, same as Dee. In fact they had worked together on a few houses.

Maybe one of the people Marisa worked for could tell me something about a party she planned to attend.

I didn't say anything to Balls or Odell about my plans. I figured I'd tell them if anything worked out.

Maybe it would.

Chapter Nine

Balls dropped me off at my house and then he and Odell went in their separate vehicles up to Duck to check neighbors where the two missing young women lived. I went up the outside steps and entered my kitchen and open area. Janey chirped her greeting and did her little head-bopping dance to welcome me home.

"Okay, Janey. Glad to see you too. But I have to go out again in a few minutes."

She said "bitch" and then "shit" as plain as anything, and followed it with the non-musical gibberish that is her usual. I've often wondered if parakeets actually think they are saying something, communicating in some way with that running-on of sounds they make. Maybe it's a secret language that only other parakeets can understand, but I have suspicions that it's nothing more than the fact that they like to make noise. And they like noise and activity around them.

I started to call Dee and tell her I wanted to stop by. But I decided against it; I would simply show up as if casually dropping by. Instead I called Elly to say hello and check again on what her schedule was for the day. I know she had told me but maybe I hadn't paid close enough attention.

"Martin's going to Lauren's birthday party this afternoon. I'll be helping out."

"Oh, yes," I said. There would be a dozen or more

children next door at Lauren's this afternoon. Elly would be busy.

"And tomorrow, you remember, Mother and Martin and I are going to Greenville to see my aunt."

"Oh, yes," I said again. "I remember."

"It'll be Monday I guess before I see you."

"I'll miss you."

"Me, too."

"Lunch Monday?"

"That would be nice." A slight pause. "Did it go all right with Agent Twiddy this morning?"

"Fine," I said. "Not a whole lot developed. Mostly talking with Odell. They're off now checking on some things."

Another pause. "And you?"

"No, I'm going to hang around here, more or less." Then I felt I should be a bit more honest. "Maybe check with Dee a bit."

"Uh-huh. Tomorrow? You flying?"

"Yes. At ten o'clock. Should be another pretty day." The month before, I'd decided to start taking flying lessons again. I had logged a few hours several years earlier back up in the Washington area, and after visiting with the instructor at the Manteo airport, figured I'd take a few more lessons. Whether I'll ever get my ticket, I don't know. But I'm enjoying it and doing it when I can.

There was the tiniest clearing of her throat. "Well now, let's see . . . there's always an ongoing investigation, there's the jazz combo you're playing with almost once a week, a bit of surf-fishing from time to time, and there're the flying lessons . . . and, oh yes, you're also a writer and supposed to be working on another book."

I could tell she was enjoying herself.

As I knew she would, she continued: "Oh, but my goodness, you've still got an open afternoon—yes, Tuesday— maybe you can take on another project. What about scuba diving? Or kite-boarding?" She grinned.

"Okay, smarty-pants," I said. "Not taking on anything else. Promise."

She laughed. Her laughter always had a musical quality to it. I could imagine her standing there, probably shaking her head. "Oh, well," she said. "I guess we women have to put up with midlife crises in our men-folk."

I could hear little Martin calling her about something. "Just a minute, Martin." Then to me, she said, "I've got to go, but see you Monday. Take good care of yourself. Be careful."

"Love you," I said, and we ended the call. I think I was still smiling to myself as I left and headed over to Dee's house.

Driving the short distance to Dee's, I thought she might be home. She preferred to work during the week when her son was in kindergarten or daycare. On Saturdays, husband Julio usually worked where he was employed with one of the air conditioning companies here at the Outer Banks. And she was home; at least her Nissan SUV was parked in the drive.

I went up the stairs and prepared to tap on the door, which wasn't necessary because she had apparently heard me arrive and stood just inside the screen door. She pushed the door open and tried a smile of greeting. "No more bad news, right?"

"No bad news," I said and smiled.

Instead of asking me in, she stepped out on the porch in the sunshine. She shaded her eyes with the palm of one hand. Her son came up behind her, holding a Nerf gun toy, bright yellow and green.

I spoke slowly so she would have a minimum of trouble following my English. "I thought, Dee, that some of the people Marisa worked for might have an idea of where this party might be that she was going to." I waited a beat or two and then said, "If you know some of where she worked, I'll go talk to the people. Maybe they can help."

It took her a moment to process my words. Then she

nodded and said, "Come in. I get the book with people names."

I followed her in. Except for some of the child play-things, the house was very neat and smelled good. Something spicy simmered on the stove. Maybe tomatoes and garlic and something else. It made my stomach rumble in appreciation.

She came back to the kitchen with a bound calendar type appointment book. She laid the book on the kitchen counter top and flipped to the back pages. Names, addresses and telephone numbers were neatly printed by hand. Among the names and addresses, I saw my own.

Dee pointed to an address a couple of spaces above mine. "I know Marisa work here long time because I work there with her some time. Talk to them." From a notepad she pulled loose a sheet and printed the name and address and telephone number. I knew exactly where the couple—Helen and Dwight Reid—lived.

I always wished I could print as neatly as Dee did. "You print—you write—real well. Good."

She looked at me an instant. Then understood. She smiled. "You a writer."

"Yes, but I type . . ." I wiggled my fingers like over a keyboard. "But I can't print neatly like you do."

"Thank you," she said. She smiled proudly and added, "*Gracias.*"

I took the slip of paper and left, but not before inhaling deeply of the aroma coming from whatever was cooking on the stove.

Driving north on the Bypass, I moved over to the left turn lane at Kitty Hawk Elementary School and made my turn onto Woods Road. I was headed to Kitty Hawk Landing. Thankfully, I didn't need directions. After a couple of turns to the right I passed Austin Cemetery and then made a left. Bearing right and then another left and I was on the road where Helen and Dwight Reid lived. Nice deep canals were on both sides of the road. From the slip of paper, I double-checked the house number and slowed, keeping my eyes out for the right one.

When I spotted the house, I parked in the driveway beside a fairly new Lexus sedan. Nice car. I mounted the steps to a high wooden porch and punched the doorbell.

I heard movement inside and then a woman of about fifty-something opened the door, a quizzical but pleasant expression on her face. "Mrs. Reid, I'm Harrison Weaver, a writer, and I'd like to talk with you a little bit about Marisa, who cleaned for you and your husband."

Her face immediately registered concern and sorrow. "Oh, what a terrible thing about her. We saw it online on *Outer Banks Voice*." She stepped back, holding the screen door open for me. "Come in." She turned her head and called, "Dwight, can you come in the living room?" She indicated the sofa for me, but we stood waiting for her husband.

From where I stood, I could see forward to the adjoining dining room and a view beyond to a back porch, canal, and a gleaming white boat at their personal dock. It looked to be a twenty-five-footer. A nice big boat.

I heard hesitant steps coming from what I assumed was the kitchen area off to the left of the dining room. Dwight Reid entered, supporting himself on a walker. He was heavyset, probably early sixties. He moved slowly, concentrating on making progress into the room; however, he smiled a greeting. His smile, though, seemed tinged with embarrassment. Still gripping the walker with his left hand, he extended his right to shake. I stepped forward and we shook hands. His grip was strong. He sank carefully into a leather chair facing the sofa. His wife watched him, and did not take her seat in another chair until he was settled.

She indicated the sofa again. "Please," she said. "This is Mr. Weaver. He wants to talk a bit about poor Marisa."

Dwight Reid kept his eyes on me. He had large eyes that stared right at me. He spoke slowly, carefully enunciating his words as if he had to practice speaking. "I know who Mr. Weaver is. Your reputation precedes you," he said, that smile still on his face. "You're a crime writer. I've followed some of your pieces and that book, too." He moved the walker a few inches to the side. "But I am curious, Mr. Weaver, since you write about crime, what's your interest in Marisa? Wasn't it an accidental drowning?"

I didn't want to get into the "suspicious death" business, so I relied on the Dee connection. "Her cousin, Dee, who works for me from time to time, asked me to talk to some people who knew Marisa." That sounded rather lame; I decided to skate a bit closer to the truth. "I believe you've met Dee also. She worked for you a few times along with Marisa, I understand, and Marisa was supposed to be going to a party that night and Dee wonders where that might have been."

Mrs. Reid spoke up. "A party? We hadn't heard anything about that."

Dwight had the barest of a bemused smile on his face. "The poor girl's body washed up on the beach. I suspect, Mr. Weaver, your interest may be more than just a favor on behalf of her cousin. I suspect you are curious about how she ended up in the ocean . . . and apparently she had been missing a couple of days." He cocked one eyebrow at me. "A party? And no one reports that she's in the ocean. And fully dressed, according to *Outer Banks Voice*."

I nodded. "You're right, Mr. Reid. While I'm doing this partly on behalf of Dee, whom I have known for three years now and consider her a friend, there are curious elements about Marisa's drowning." I sat straighter on the edge of the sofa seat. I couldn't help but wonder about his interest in and his knowledge about the drowning. "I'm most interested in where this party might have been. Who was having it?"

"I wish we could help you on that, Mr. Weaver. Unfortunately at this stage of life, Barbara and I don't host parties, nor do we attend many." He chuckled. "Although attending a party with an attractive young woman like Marisa does have its appeal."

Mrs. Wright frowned at his last remark but remained silent.

He raised his chin toward me, that pleasant expression still on his face. "I don't mean to sound even the least bit like I am not treating this as a very tragic happening. And maybe some of the other people she worked for may be able to give guidance about this alleged party."

Mrs. Wright spoke up. "He could talk to the Cleaves except they are up in Maine this week." She sat with her hands folded tightly in her lap, her back straight. "Marisa worked for them too. They're brother and sister. They live on the other side of the street, a couple of houses up."

"Oh, yes," Dwight said. "But whether they would know anything about a party one of the 'hired help' might be attending is doubtful." He used fingers of both hands to signal quote marks around *hired help*.

Then Mrs. Wright rose and stepped back in the kitchen and came back with a slip of paper with a name and address written on it. "This is a friend of mine that I recommended Marisa to. She lives in Southern Shores and maybe she can help you."

I stood. "Thank you, and thank you so much for allowing me to come unannounced, and for chatting with me a bit."

Mrs. Reid remained standing. Dwight kept his seat. I raised one hand toward the windows that looked out from the dining room toward the backyard and the canal. "That's nice boat you have there, Mr. Reid. What a twenty-five-footer?"

"Thank you," he said. "Yes, it has served us well. We've used it fishing a great deal. Mostly up around Wright Memorial Bridge or down to Manns Harbor Bridge. Barbara is the better fisherman." That smile remained. "Twenty-one feet, actually. You have a boat?"

"Yes, I have an eighteen-foot Ranger."

"Ranger is a good boat." He pulled the walker over closer, put both hands on it as if preparing to rise. "If you're interested in boats, you should see the one the Cleaves have. Thirty-five or thirty-six feet. Sleeps six or eight." He shook his head. "They even have a captain and a mate or two when they take the boat out for any distance. Real trips, too, like all the way up to Maine to their cottage there."

"Must be nice," I said. Then I thanked them again and gave one of my cards and asked them to call if they thought of anything else. I took a step toward Mr. Reid as he struggled to stand. His wife stood at the ready, also.

"I'm fine," he said.

But it pained me to watch him.

When I left their house, I drove down the road a short distance and checked out the Cleaves's home—easily the most elegant on the street. I caught a glimpse of the boat docked behind their house. From what I could see of it, it looked like a damn yacht. I'd seen bigger, but still, it was pretty flashy for a backyard boat.

I decided to give the Southern Shores people a shot, the ones whose address Mrs. Reid had given me. They were most gracious—Mrs. Reid had called in advance. But they were no more helpful than the Reids. Apparently Marisa came in, did her work, chatting very little, and departed.

When I left Southern Shores, I called Balls on his cell to see if they had had any luck.

"Zilch. Nada," he said. "Nobody knows anything. At the house of the two up in Duck, one neighbor did say that they saw a lot of cars going and coming at the house, but nothing of any consequence. Odell is pretty frustrated." I heard him sigh. "I'm going home. On my way now."

I drove on south along the Bypass to the street that leads toward my house. I was frustrated, too. And I knew Balls was. I could hear it in his voice.

Well, maybe something would develop when we least expect it. That seems like the case more often than not.

Meanwhile, I was going to eat a late lunch, take a nap, and think about going flying tomorrow morning.

Chapter Ten

Sunday morning I was up early. Another beautiful day. I stepped out on the deck, breathed in the fresh air, the hint of salt coming off the ocean. There was virtually no wind. Perfect day for a flying lesson.

After a quick bite to eat and checking on Janey, I headed out in my Subaru toward Manteo and the airport on the west side of town. Traffic was light that early Sunday morning, even though it was picking up as weekenders began to head to homes north of the Outer Banks.

It was not quite eight-thirty when I parked at the airport. My instructor, Sam, was inside leaning her elbows on the counter talking to the young man on duty that morning. Her full name is Samantha Inez Davis, but everyone calls her Sam. She's about five-seven, high cheekbones, very green eyes, and stylishly short reddish hair. She could be a model. That morning she wore knee-length khaki shorts and a collared-tee, with her flying school logo on the pocket. I believe she has a steady boyfriend, who is in construction of some type, and not a pilot. There are plenty of guys around the airport who would love to take his place.

And she's a hell of a good pilot and instructor. I feel lucky to have her. This would be my third lesson with her. She knows that I logged about eight hours of instruction a few years ago in Northern Virginia. Then no flying at all until a month ago when I took what we call "a dollar ride" with Sam and signed up.

I said good morning to one of the young pilots who had come in. When Sam heard me speak, she turned around and smiled. "Well, here's my fellow-flyer. Ready to go up and see what's happening in the skies today?"

"Absolutely," I said. Actually, I was always a tad nervous when we were about to get started on a lesson. Maybe it was more like a controlled anxiousness; it was not fear, but the heart beat a bit faster.

"Let's go," she said.

I followed her out to the right where a Cessna 172 was parked. The plane looked good with the sun hitting it and the waters of the Croatan Sound beyond, and the sun glancing off the waters too.

"Okay," she said, "even though Jesse just took this plane up for a quick spin, I want you to make a preflight check anyway." She insisted on this, and instructed me to do it in the same sequence each time so that it would become ingrained.

I began my walk-around at the pilot's door by removing the pitot cover under the leading edge of the wing. Made sure it was not clogged. Didn't want it to impede a reading of airspeed.

Ahead of the pilot door, I checked the other airspeed vent hole, and then went to the wing leading edge near the wing root and used my mouth to suck slightly on the small square hole to activate the stall warning horn. Wanted to make sure it worked.

There was a little glass vial in a pouch behind the left seat and I inserted it in the small fuel drain hole beneath the pilot-side wing. Checked it to make sure no water was in the fuel. A bit of water could ruin your day. The low-lead 100-octane gasoline for the Cessna is tinted blue, and water, being heavier than gasoline and colorless, would show at the bottom of the vial.

Next, I checked the pilot-side aileron's connection and hinges and moved it up and down to make sure it had free travel. Walking back to the tail I checked for free movement and tight cables connections on both the vertical rudder and horizontal elevator. At the same time, I was inspecting the aircraft for any dings or for any evident low pressure in any one of the three tires.

Finished the walk-around by taking a fuel sample from the starboard wing tank and checking the aileron.

I opened the rectangular inspection door on the engine cowling and checked the oil level. Closing the cowling door, I felt the leading edge of the prop for any nicks. I made sure the air intakes in the nose were clear all the way inside the cowling. I made sure the connections to the nose wheel were okay.

I glanced at Sam, who had been watching me steadily the whole time.

"Let's get in, check everything there. Then go for a ride."

I nodded and climbed in the left side door and buckled up. The interior of the aircraft smelled vaguely of sun-warmed vinyl and gasoline. We put on headsets and Sam flipped the switch so we could talk to each other once the engine was running.

Sam had me make sure the altimeter, which measures air pressure and can vary from day to day and even hour to hour, was set properly at airport elevation. Also, I set the directional gyro at the same heading as the wet magnetic compass mounted atop the instrument panel.

"Okay, Sport, start the engine," Sam said.

I opened my door a bit and called out, "Clear prop." Another safety precaution even though we knew no one was near the front of the plane.

I started the engine. It caught right away. I eased off the toe brakes at the top of each rudder pedal and began a slow roll toward the far northeast end of the runway. A light wind from the south. We'd be taking off toward the Croatan Sound.

As always, when the process started my adrenalin worked overtime.

I eased the Cessna up to the hold line just before the runway. Pressing firmly on the toe brakes, I did an engine run-up to 2500 rpm, and turned on the carburetor heat and cycled the magneto switches to make sure both worked.

Manteo is not a controlled airport but just the same pilots announce that they are planning to take off. Sam did this, then grinned at me and said, "Let's go for a ride."

I nodded. I felt excited. Maybe a little nervous. I checked both ways for traffic, and eased off the brakes and applied a bit more power. We rolled forward, and I steered right onto the taxiway. I still had to concentrate on guiding the aircraft with my feet on the rudder petals and resist the temptation to try to steer by turning the yoke as if I were in an automobile.

In position, it looked like the runway stretched out in front of me forever. Braking firmly to hold the plane in place, I advanced the rpm until the Cessna shook from the power.

Sam nodded. "Let's go," she said.

With engine roaring, I released my toes from the brakes. Quickly we rolled forward, picking up speed. I was not expert at keeping the aircraft straight forward without a few wobbles right and left; then I got more of the hang of it as we went faster and faster down the runway. In what seemed like a short distance I felt us lifting off the ground and gave the slightest tug back on the yoke and we rose into the air, heading out above the sun-sparkled waters of the Croatan Sound.

Airborne. A wonderful feeling. I breathed in happily. I may have been grinning.

At about three hundred feet above the sound, I did a gentle bank to the right and we swung back toward land.

"That was smooth," Sam said. Then I know I grinned.

"Climb to about seven hundred and head mostly north. Straight and level."

I nodded. Then said, "Roger," like a real pilot. Like in the movies.

I kept glancing right and left to make sure I kept my wing tips even with the horizon, and also to make sure no traffic was coming our way. We passed over Roanoke Sound, then up toward Kitty Hawk. I could see the Wright Memorial Bridge up ahead to my right. I'd leveled off at seven hundred feet.

"After you cross the Currituck Sound, bank to the right and follow along the beach south." She smiled at me. "And don't say 'roger.' Just do it."

I made my turn and she said, "Check your altitude. Don't lose altitude when you turn."

Checking the altimeter, it read five-fifty. I fed the engine a bit more power and pulled back a tad on the yoke. By the time we headed along the coastline we were up to seven hundred again.

We flew down the coast all the way to Oregon Inlet. She had me make a turn back north, and I was careful to keep the nose up a bit so we didn't lose altitude. Coming back to Bodie Lighthouse, Sam had me circle around it, banking rather sharply. I didn't lose altitude, but I concentrated on it.

"Good," she said. "Head toward Wanchese—see it over there—and then we'll line up with the airport."

I was really enjoying it and I felt more comfortable. I could see the village of Wanchese and the coastline there, the boat-building facilities.

"Okay," Sam said, "line up toward the airport."

The airport was to my left. It appeared tiny and faraway. It wasn't, of course, but it looked that way. Speaking over the radio to the airport, Sam told the young man there that we planned to be coming in for a landing.

After jockeying around with a couple of adjusting turns, Sam said to me, "Line up and begin a descent."

I wasn't sure how much she wanted me to do. I became a little tense.

"Cut back some on the rpm, begin to nose down," she said.

I nodded.

"Don't worry," she said, glancing at me. "I'll take it as we come in but keep your hands lightly on the yoke so you can feel what I'm doing."

Our altitude was dropping, and it seemed to me like the runway was coming up faster than I thought it would.

"Give me fifteen degrees of flap," she said.

I glanced at the control panel and moved the flaps down a notch.

"One more," she said.

The runway got closer. The trees at the northeast end of the runway appeared larger.

"Give me less rpm."

I could feel the Cessna slowing and sinking.

"I've got it now," she said.

I released my grip on the yoke. I hadn't realized I was holding it so tight. Resting my fingers lightly on it, I was glad to be turning it over to her. The runway came up faster. I felt her ease back on the yoke and we touched down— smoothly. She applied the brakes and cut back even more on the engine. She taxied to almost a stop.

She said, "Okay, sport, you take it and park it."

I applied the brakes, then engaged right rudder and the aircraft swung around. With a bit more juice to the engine, I managed to get us parked on the apron to the side of the terminal. It may not have been the smoothest job of parking, but I got us there and she nodded for me to cut the engine. It suddenly seemed very quiet and I took a deep breath.

"You did good," she said. "I believe you could have brought it in."

I shook my head. "I don't know . . ."

We unbuckled and got out. Jesse, one of the young pilots who worked for Sam, came toward us. A couple and a young child followed him.

"Jesse has a tour," Sam said. They spoke to each other and I looked back at the plane. Yes, I was proud, and it probably showed a bit in the way I walked with Sam back to the terminal.

"Let's update your logbook," she said. "And set a date for your next lesson."

Inside the terminal we sat side-by-side and she took my logbook. "Those previous lessons were a while back," she said. "But almost eight hours. Good. You're coming along." She entered the time in my book and wrote "straight and level flight, turns." She consulted a calendar she had in her small bag. "Depending on the weather, and your schedule, how about Thursday early morning?"

"Fine," I said. Privately I wondered what might be happening with any sort of progress being made on the missing young women, but I didn't say anything further.

We stood and shook hands. I prepared to leave when she said, "What are you writing about now?"

That took me by surprise. She knew, of course, that I'm a crime writer, but we hadn't talked about it at all . . . until now. "Oh, trying to finish up a book dealing with that business about the Bear Woman." I referred to a case I'd worked on and written about back in the spring. It was a case my editor, Rose, wanted me to do a book on.

As she put her calendar away, she said, "I thought you might be working on those missing girls."

News spreads fast here at the Outer Banks, especially among the locals. My inclination is usually to be rather circumspect when a statement is made I wasn't expecting. With luck, I find out a bit more about what the person is thinking before I say too much. "I've heard about a couple of missing young women," I admitted.

"Robert—you know, my boyfriend—thinks there may be more than just those two."

She had my attention. "Yes?"

"He's in construction, and he had this young woman—a really good worker—been with him all summer. She was from the Ukraine or somewhere, and suddenly she disappeared. Couple or three days ago. Just like that. Not like her. No one knows where she is."

Sam leaned in a little closer and spoke softly. "Robert thinks it could be human trafficking, like he's been reading about."

Chapter Eleven

Before I left the airport, I talked a bit more with Sam about Robert's suspicions about human trafficking and his missing worker. I told her that I expected that Chief Deputy Odell Wright would probably like to talk with him. Actually, I knew damn well that Odell would talk with him.

Driving through Manteo, I decided to eat an early lunch, so I stopped at Darrell's, took a booth, and got the sliced pork and sweet potatoes luncheon special. I thought about what Sam had said about human trafficking, but I spent most of my time reliving my flying lesson. It was exhilarating. But truthfully, I wasn't convinced I would pursue it enough to get my private license. To do it right, and be proficient enough so that you're not a hazard to yourself—or others— you need to devote a lot of time to it, and I wasn't sure I wanted to invest that much time, not with everything else I was involved with—the demands of writing and playing a bit of music with Jim Watson and combo, a bit of fishing thrown in, some golf, not to mention spending time with Elly.

Oh, well, I was enjoying it so far. I'd pull a Scarlett O'Hara and think about that tomorrow.

When I got home, I trudged up the stairs, spoke to Janey and treated her with a sprig of millet seed. Maybe it was the nice lunch settling on my stomach or the aftermath of ex-pending emotional energy and concentration on the flying, but I suddenly felt weary, tired. Actually, sort of sleepy. Well, heck, I'd lie down and read, maybe doze off. It was, after all, Sunday afternoon and Elly and her mother and Martin were in Greenville. I read every day for at least an hour. Not like the late Pat Conroy who aimed at reading two hundred pages a day, but I do get in quite a few pages—and, depending on the book, read them critically as a means of improving my own writing; a never-ending process, never getting good enough.

An hour or so later when I got up, I felt groggy and almost wished I hadn't lain down. Oh, well, a cup of French roast coffee should do the trick. When I took the coffee out on the deck, I checked the time. Almost four. I watched a few puffy clouds come across the sky from the south. The sun felt good, and a light breeze brought in a scent of pine from the trees on the left side of my house.

I was beginning to come around.

The phone rang. I set my coffee down on the little wrought iron table beside my chair, heaved myself up and got inside the sliding glass door by the third ring. I didn't recognize the number on caller ID but I picked up to answer anyway. And I heard the caller click off before I could speak. The line went dead.

I went back outside. My coffee was still warm. I like it really hot. I thought about zapping it in the microwave but figured it was okay as it was. I plopped back down in the chair.

The phone rang again.

"Shit," I muttered. (So maybe that's partly where Janey gets her language.) I went back inside. It was the same number. But this time I answered more quickly.

The line was still open. I could tell someone was there. I could hear breathing. I said hello, again, and waited.

I was about to hang up.

Then, "Mr. Weaver?" It was a man's voice, probably young, but sounding tenuous.

This didn't sound like a telemarketing call. Something about his voice. Just the same, I never respond to the caller's question without asking one of my own. So I said, "Who's calling?"

There was no response except for his breathing. I think he cleared his throat. I was about to launch into a repeat of who's calling, or maybe even slam the phone in its cradle. But something made me stop, wait a bit more.

His words came out in a rush, his voice unsteady. "I can tell you what happened to those girls. And the other ones."

Now it was I who took a breath. I gripped the phone tightly, as if I could squeeze more out of him by putting pressure on the handset. "Tell me," I said. My voice didn't sound as it did normally.

"Not on the phone," he said. "I don't want them to know."

"The girls?" I said.

"No. The other people."

I tried to get control of the conversation. "Why are you offering to tell me?"

"You write about stuff. I've read you. You maybe can do something about it."

"What about the police? The authorities?"

"No," he said, his voice louder. "Meet me at five o'clock at that little beach area south of Jockey's Ridge. You know where it is?

"Yes, I know. But why can't you tell me now."

"Will you meet me? Alone? No one with you."

I took a deep breath. I was torn between wanting to follow him on this and worried at the same time there might be something—well, hazardous—about agreeing to meet him. But I knew I couldn't resist. A part of my nature. The reporter smelling a big story?

"Okay," I said. "Five o'clock." I glanced at my watch. About an hour from now. Then I added, "But I need to know who you are."

"No you don't," he said, and the line went dead.

I stood there and exhaled a full breath of air as if I hadn't breathed for a while. Then I immediately punched in Balls' cell phone number. The call went straight to voice mail. "Call me on my land line or cell as soon as you can. Got an anonymous call from some guy who claims he knows what happened to those girls. He wants me to meet him in about an hour just south of Jockey's Ridge." I slowed down my speech. "I'm going to call Odell now and alert him. Guy wants me to be alone."

No luck getting Odell at the sheriff's office. I didn't have his cell number (which I vowed to get, and I knew he would give me). His home phone was not listed. I spoke with the dispatcher and asked him to contact Odell and tell him it was urgent that he call me. I supplied my cell number, although I assumed he had captured it anyway. Maybe not, for he had me repeat the number to make sure he had it.

I kept glancing at my watch, and I paced back out on the deck, paused for a sip of the cold coffee. I walked back and forth. Then I made myself sit down. A moment later I got up and took my coffee cup inside and washed it. Gave Janey fresh water and replenished her seeds.

At my desk, which is really the dinette table that is just off the kitchen and facing the south windows over the deck, I opened the second drawer of my three-drawer wooden file cabinet and catchall. Took out my mini recorder; figured I'd take that in my pocket. With a shake of my head, I even thought about taking my .32 caliber revolver, which I store wrapped in an old hand towel in the bottom drawer of my bedside table. I haven't fired that thing in about three years. Keep it cleaned, oiled and loaded, though, just in case. Well, going into a situation that I'm not sure about so maybe not such a bad idea to stick that little pea shooter under my front seat. But the guy on the phone sounded more scared and nervous than dangerous. However, I knew a frightened and nervous person could sometimes be out of control and thus present a real threat.

At seventeen minutes before five I went downstairs and got in my car. Driving out to the Bypass I headed south toward Jockey's Ridge. As usual, I caught a red light at First Street and again at Landing Drive at Lowe's. Managed to hit the rest of the lights on green, and made fairly good time despite the heavy tourist traffic.

Jockey's Ridge came into view. Even though it's the largest sand dune on the East Coast, depending on the sand-carrying wind its height varies. There were only two or three tiny figures at the pinnacle. No hang gliders. The sun was getting lower in the west, but there was still plenty of light and would be for two or three more hours.

Shortly beyond the dune, I turned right onto the small road and headed toward the sound. About a quarter of a mile later, I turned right again at the tiny road that led to a small parking area. A number of young mothers and others used this little alcove and "beach" area that is accessed through a path over dunes to the shallow sound. Children can wade out several yards into the clear water and the sand covered bottom and still hardly be in water up to their waists. At the far side of the parking area there's a nature trail through a low maritime forest. Lovely spot.

But it didn't seem all that lovely to me that evening.

My breathing was a bit shallow and I slowed my car and stared straight ahead.

A fairly new Ford pickup truck was the only other vehicle. It had to be his, my anonymous caller's. But I couldn't see him. I was only about ten yards from his truck, but my seat was lower than the cab of the truck.

I cut my engine and got out slowly, eyes sweeping the truck, the rest of the parking lot, the woods, and the path to the water.

Slowly I walked toward the truck. Two yards, three, four yards closer. Eyes alternately on the truck and the surrounding area.

Now I was close enough to see into the top part of the

truck's cab, the steering wheel and windshield. I got closer.

Then I saw.

I froze, sucked in a breath.

He was stretched out on the seat, his head toward the passenger door, one knee on the floorboard, the other leg partly extended as if he prepared to try to get out the passenger door.

He hadn't made it, though.

There was blood. A lot of blood.

A quick look at him up close through the driver's window, which was down. I didn't touch anything, but I leaned forward and peered inside. Blood had come from what was probably a gunshot to the head and another one in his back.

Then I pulled back from the truck and turned my head to the right, left and over my shoulders. A moment of fear in case whoever did this might still be nearby.

I felt for my cell phone, although I knew it was in the back pocket. I had to call 911 but I also knew the first thing the dispatcher would want to know was whether the victim was still alive. Going quickly to the other side of the truck, I pulled out a folded piece of paper towel I use instead of a cloth handkerchief. With the paper towel on the handle, I carefully opened the passenger door.

His eyes were partially open, and dead looking, staring dully at nothing. Steeling myself, I extended the fingers of my left hand and, trying to avoid blood, I felt his neck for a pulse. There was none, as I was sure there would not be. His skin was pliable and, while not really warm, was not totally cold either.

He hadn't been dead long. I stepped back, wiping my fingers vigorously with the paper towel, and extracted my cell phone. But as I prepared to punch in 911 the phone rang and vibrated—and startled me. Made me jump. It was Odell.

"You wanted me to call you?" he said.

I swallowed before I spoke. "Odell . . . we got a body."

Chapter Twelve

After briefly filling Odell in on the situation and the anonymous phone call from the person I assumed was the same one who was now the victim, I went back to my Subaru, opened the door and sat on the edge of the seat, one foot on the floorboard, the other outside on the ground. Maybe it was overly precautious, but I retrieved my .32 revolver from under the front seat, took it out of the towel and held it in my lap. It made me feel more secure, safer, more in control.

Odell would be making all the necessary calls and speeding out here himself.

In what couldn't have been more than five minutes I heard sirens. I listened, relieved to hear them.

The first vehicle to arrive—and pulled in quickly, too— was a cruiser from the Nags Head Police Department. Two officers got out immediately. I stood and took a couple of steps toward them. They eyed me without smiling. "In the cab of that truck there," I said, tossing my head in the direction of the Ford pickup.

One of the officers stayed close to me. He kept his eyes on me. "Why'd you come out here?" he said.

"To meet him," I said. "And that's the way I found him."

He glanced at the open door of my Subaru. The revolver lay on the seat. "That yours?" he said. He kept his eyes on me. His right hand was at the ready near his holstered weapon.

"Well, yes," I said. I tried something of a smile. Didn't quite make it. "It hasn't been fired—in about three years."

He went to my car, extracted a handkerchief from his back pocket and lifted the revolver gingerly from the handle.

"Careful," I said. "It's loaded."

He sniffed the barrel. I'm sure he smelled nothing but clean oil. It had obviously not been fired. He laid the gun back on the seat. "I guess you got a permit for that?" he said.

I nodded. "Oh, yes." *I think I've got a permit somewhere. Not sure I even needed one. Been a long time.*

The other officer returned to where we stood. He appeared to be trying to keep his face neutral and not display emotions I knew he felt viewing that bloody body. "You touch anything?" he said to me.

I shook my head. "I felt for a pulse on his neck. Opened the door with a paper towel. Didn't touch anything else or disturb anything."

Then I heard more sirens and the Dare County emergency vehicle arrived, with Odell in a sheriff department's cruiser right behind it. Then another Dare County deputy pulled up. We were getting crowded with vehicles.

Odell came straight to me, shook hands briefly, and we began conferring softly. The Nags Head officers appeared to lose interest in me. They stood to one side.

The two medics stepped out of the ambulance, donning latex gloves and approached the pickup truck. They glanced first at Odell and he nodded a go-ahead. I knew both of the medics: Duncan—my confidential body-spotter—and Pam. In addition to working as an EMT, Duncan moonlighted as a first mate on some of the charter boats. They looked very grim. They went to the passenger side of the pickup. They weren't there long. Duncan came back to Odell and said, "Expired." Then he said, "We'll wait around until you give the word."

Odell said, "Dr. Willis will be here soon." Willis was the long-time acting coroner/medical examiner. For full autopsy, however, I knew the body would be sent to Greenville.

Odell motioned for the other deputy. "Camera," Odell said. The deputy, a fairly new one named Duvall, went back to the cruiser and retrieved a camera from the trunk.

"From both sides," Odell said. "Up close, too. And the interior."

Duvall didn't smile. "Yes, sir," he said.

"I'll be there in a minute," Odell said. Then he turned back to me. "Exactly what did he say when he called."

I wished I had written it down. "Very little, actually. Main thing he said, the thing that really got my attention, was that he could tell me what happened to those girls."

"Anything else?"

"He wanted me to meet him here at five o'clock. He wouldn't give his name. Wanted me to be sure I came alone." I tried to recall more of conversation. "He wouldn't tell me anything over the phone . . . and he seemed nervous, agitated . . . and fearful."

Odell said, "He obviously had reason to be fearful." He appeared to be thinking of something. "You recognize him?"

I shook my head. "Not at all."

"I'll check his ID when Duvall gets through with the photographs." From a shirt pocket he produced a small spiral notepad. He jotted down the license number of the truck, returned to his cruiser, and picked up his radio. I could hear him talking, and then he was silent, waiting. In less than three minutes, he said, "Yes, got it," and he wrote something in his notepad.

Another Nags Head police cruiser pulled into the area and parked well to one side away from the ambulance. Two more officers came up to the first two and began talking quietly. I couldn't hear what they were saying. But one of the officers took up a position at the roadway entrance to prevent any curious citizens from approaching.

Odell went to the pickup and told Duvall that he probably had enough photos. Both doors of the truck were open now. The two windows had been down. I watched Odell reach in with a gloved hand and retrieve a wallet from the left back pocket of the victim. He flipped it open and apparently checked the driver's license. He dropped the wallet into a clear plastic evidence bag he had pulled from his side pocket. He handed the bag to Duvall. "Hang on to this."

Then more to himself than to me, he said, "Be glad when Dr. Willis gets here." Then he added, "Looks like he was shot at least three times. In the face, the back, and side of his head."

"No shell casings?" I said.

"Haven't seen any yet." Then again almost to himself, "Shooter either used a revolver or he picked up the casings." He glanced over at me. "Somebody didn't want him telling you what happened to those girls."

"But how did someone know he was going to . . . to talk?"

"Monitored his call. Listened in. Maybe on a phone they'd given him." He added under his breath, "Whoever *they* is." He compressed his lips, frowning. "Didn't see a cell phone. Unless he's lying on it. Search the cab better when the body is moved. Maybe the shooter took the cell along with the casings."

Odell stood staring at the victim. "ID lists him as Thomas A. Findley. Truck's registered in his name."

Duncan stood nearby awaiting the word to remove the body, and he obviously heard Odell mention the victim's name. Duncan stepped closer. "I thought I recognized him. 'Tommy' is how I've known him. Didn't know his last name. But I couldn't be sure who it was because his face is sort of messed up. But he's worked freelance as a deckhand on some of the charter fishing boats. Handling the reels, bringing in the fish, cleaning them, catering to the customers, bringing them drinks and stuff. Haven't seen him for a while. Figured he'd gotten himself a steady job on a boat."

"Thanks," Odell said. I could tell he thought about trying to trace down where Tommy Findley was working. Might be a good solid lead. Then Odell added to Duncan: "Won't be much longer. Soon as Dr. Willis gets here, we'll wrap it up and you can take the body."

Duncan nodded. "No problem," he said. "We're on the clock." He stepped back to speak to his partner, Pam.

When Duncan had gone, Odell studied my face. "You thinking what I'm thinking?"

"Yes."

He pursed his lips, and slowly moved his head up and down. "You're thinking he was on that alleged party boat, the one our drowning victim was on, and the one those other two young women were on."

"That's exactly what I'm thinking," I said. "Now all we got to do is find the boat."

"Yeah," Odell said, "as if that's gonna be easy."

"And if we do, that'll probably be only the beginning."

Chapter Thirteen

It wasn't more than five minutes before Dr. Willis arrived in his dusty sedan and, as usual, a little dusty himself. He wore a white dress shirt that looked like he'd taken a nap in it. He never managed to get his shirts tucked in properly. His tie was loosened and a bit askew. Not smiling, he approached Odell, nodded, his eyes on the pickup truck.

Dr. Willis carried a small black medical bag of some sort. I wasn't at all sure what could be in the bag. There was certainly nothing that could help the young man sprawled bloody and dead in the front seat of his truck.

Odell and Dr. Willis walked slowly toward the truck, with Odell indicating they should approach the passenger side. Dr. Willis set his bag on the front right fender of the vehicle and extracted latex gloves, worked them onto his hands. He had spoken quietly to Odell, and I drifted closer so I could hear. Everyone else had stayed back.

As I got closer, I stopped because my cell phone chirped and vibrated in my side pocket. It was Balls.

"I can't even spend the afternoon off with my wife without you bugging me about something you've got going on." He sounded gruff, but I knew he wasn't. It was just Balls.

"Give Lorraine by best," I said, "but we've got a body here." Then I gave him a quick rundown.

He was quiet, listening, Then he said, "Odell tied up?"

"He's with Dr. Willis, who just got here." I got Odell's attention and mouthed that it was Balls. "Let me see if I can get him," I said.

With two strides, Odell was beside me and I handed him my phone. They talked and I watched Dr. Willis.

Odell signed off and he handed me my phone. "He'll be down first thing in the morning. Said for you to be at my office, too."

I nodded.

Odell moved back to the passenger side of the truck. Dr. Willis leaned partly inside the cab. His efforts untucked his shirt even more. He straightened to stand close in at the opened door. He rolled his shoulders and pressed a hand against the small of his back. "Not dead long," he mumbled. "An hour or two at the most."

Dr. Willis had pushed the man's shoulder back so he could inspect the chest area. "Shot three times. Small caliber. Once here under the left jawbone. That bullet exited below the right eye. No other exit wounds. So those two bullets are still in him. One in the back and one in the lower left side back of the head. Either one of these could have been fatal."

Odell leaned closer. "The one in the cheek exited?"

"Yep. Maybe still here in the cab."

Standing behind and to one side of Odell, I glanced around the cab as best I could. There at the lower edge of the right side of the windshield there was a small spider-web crack like a rock had flown up and hit it, but then I saw the crack was on the inside; and there wedged almost in the vent at the bottom of the windshield a tiny object with a dull sheen.

I pointed and said to Odell, "A bullet?"

"That's it," Odell said, and he carefully picked up the spent bullet with his gloved hand, being careful not to scratch it further against the vent; he dropped it into a small plastic bag. "It's a twenty-two, looks like."

Dr. Willis had that sad expression on his face. "Not anything more I can do here at the scene. They'll have to do their business in Greenville." He took a deep breath and I realized how weary he appeared. Viewing as much death as he did, it had to take its toll.

"Can the medics take the body now?" Odell said.

"Yep." Dr. Willis retrieved his little black satchel and peeled off his gloves, stuck them in a side pocket on the satchel. He trudged back to his sedan.

Odell stood back as Duncan and Pam came up with the gurney and body bag. "I want to make sure there's nothing in the cab we need to get," Odell said. "A cell phone would be nice. But I've got a feeling there's not going to be one." He called to Deputy Duvall: "Go ahead and get a tow truck to get this pickup. Get it impounded." More to himself he muttered. "Get forensic guys to go over it tomorrow." He looked at me. "I told you Balls will be down early in the morning?"

"Yes, you did. I'll be there."

"Oh, that's right." He seemed distracted. "He said he wanted to talk about maybe having to involve the Feds."

"FBI?"

He nodded. "He feels we may be dealing with kidnapping, and that's federal."

"Well, if it involves trafficking, that's got to start with kidnapping." Then I thought about it and corrected myself. "No, they could go voluntarily before they realize they can't get away."

"Yeah." He shook his head as in disbelief. "Human trafficking, I'm sure. And it's not a one-time thing, I don't think. It's organized and it's extensive."

"And serious," I said. "Deadly serious," and I inclined my head toward the ambulance where the medics had stowed the gurney holding the body of Thomas A. Findley.

Chapter Fourteen

When I got home it was almost dark. Cutting the engine on the Subaru, I sat there a moment or so. Thinking about the day. Then I retrieved the revolver I'd rewrapped in the cotton towel, got out, locked the car, and went slowly up the outside stairs to my kitchen door. Smiling wryly to myself over the way I was trudging along, I felt like I moved with the same weariness that Dr. Willis had displayed. Been a long day. A very long day.

I wanted to call Elly, but I thought I ought to get a bit more vim in my spirit before I did. She could read me well, and she would read weariness in my soul. And that was it. A weariness of the soul. There was evil out there and even after as many crimes as I'd covered and written about, I was still punched in the soul by it.

How could humans do these things? I shook my head and opened the kitchen door and tried to acknowledge Janey's happy chirping as a greeting to welcome me home.

It was well after eight before Elly, her mother, and Martin got home from Greenville. Elly was busy trying to get an overly tired and fussy Martin ready for bed. We agreed we'd try to have lunch tomorrow. I didn't go into what had happened late that afternoon, but I did tell her that the flying lesson with Sam went well. When she got to the courthouse in the morning, she'd find out soon enough about

Tommy Findley's murder. I'd spell out more of it at lunch, I was sure.

I went to bed fairly early and waked up early, too. I half-expected to hear from Balls this morning, insisting that I buy him breakfast. But then he probably wasn't in the mood for a get-together before he made a nonstop trip from Elizabeth City to the Dare County Courthouse. All business today.

After a quick bite to eat and a shower, I donned khakis, a collared golf shirt, and boat shoes. More businesslike attire than usual for me—and others—here at the Outer Banks in late summer.

It was only a little after eight-thirty when I parked on Sir Walter Raleigh Street across from the courthouse. From the front porch of the courthouse I saw Balls' Thunderbird parked in one of the reserved spots on Budleigh Street closest to the corner.

I went in quickly. Elly's office is the first one on the left. She was already at work and she saw me. I raised a hand in greeting, ready to hurry on, but she said, "I'd like to talk with you . . . about late yesterday afternoon." Uh-oh. I could tell by the tone of her voice she already knew all of the details from Mabel. Mabel was a friend of both of us and had been with the sheriff's office for something like a hundred years.

"Catch up with you a little later," I said, giving a big, innocent smile. Not sure it worked, though.

She cocked her head at me, a bit of a reprimanding frown on her face.

I scurried down the hall and up the backstairs to the sheriff's offices. Big, bear-like Sheriff Eugene Albright stood in the doorway of his office speaking to Mabel. His body practically filled the doorway. He acknowledged me with a short smile. "It never seems to stop, does it?" he said, with a sad shake of his head. He's a kindly man, basically a gentle soul, who would much rather counsel a potential lawbreaker than arrest him.

Mabel held message notes in her hand, ready to deliver

them to Albright. First, though, she said to me, "They're in there." She indicated Odell's office. She wore one of her long skirts, a loose-fitting top, and her usual black rubber-sole shoes, the ones that helped her ankles. Some months earlier she announced she was utterly and entirely through with any sort of dieting forever.

I tapped on Odell's door, opened it and went inside. He sat behind his desk; Balls was tilted back against the wall in a straight-back chair, the front legs of the chair off the floor.

Odell indicated the other chair near his desk.

Balls said, "You oversleep?"

"And good morning to you," I said.

Odell said, "I was giving Agent Twiddy a rundown of yesterday."

To me, Balls said, "Tell me exactly what this victim said to you when he called."

"Actually, he called twice. The first time he hung up without saying anything. But I could tell someone was on the line in the beginning. Then he called back a minute or so later. Sounded nervous, afraid—and he had a right to be."

Eyes cast down as if studying his hands, Balls said, "Someone monitored his call. Probably cell phone."

"That's what I figured," I said.

"We didn't find a cell," Odell said. "Wasn't one in the truck."

"Figures," Balls said.

I continued. "He wouldn't give his name. Said he could tell me what happened to those girls." I paused a moment, thinking. "I think he said 'those girls' but he might have said 'the girls,' like there were more than those two."

Odell sadly shook his head. "It's a ring, I'm sure. Organized. A real operation. Not just a couple of rogues. Someone steps out of line, like Findley, and he's eliminated."

Balls appeared to weigh that statement. He chewed lightly on his lower lip. "Agreed." Then he looked at me. I couldn't read his expression, but if I had to guess it was one of concern. "Good thing you didn't arrive there five or ten minutes earlier." He made what sounded like a mirthless chortle. "Don't need a double homicide."

"Yes, I thought about that." I swallowed and thought about what might have been a deadly confrontation. Then I forced myself to dismiss that, and said, "I didn't see anyone coming toward me on that little road behind Jockey's Ridge. But, hell, I might very well have passed the shooter on the highway and never would have noticed."

"Okay, what now?" Balls said, although I was sure he already had plans for what's next.

Odell said, "I got blowups of Findley's photo from his driver's license. Given copies to Duvall and Dorsey to take around to the marinas, see if any of the dock masters or boat owners know where he was working most recently."

"His next of kin?" Balls asked.

"The sheriff has taken care of that," Odell said. "A stepmother over near Columbia. No one else."

Balls again: "Media?"

"Word hasn't gotten out as fast as I thought it would," Odell said. "Something online in the *Outer Banks Voice,* and Linda Shackleford has already called this morning. Albright promised her I'd talk with her about nine-thirty or so."

Linda was one of the reporters I knew best, and I liked her. She was a long-time friend of Elly's too. She recently had moved from *The Coastland Times* to the *Outer Banks Sentinel*, where she was doing some really good work. In depth news features. Both papers are local.

We were all three quiet for a minute or more. I think I knew what was coming next.

Balls cleared his throat, leaned forward so that all four legs of the chair bumped on the floor. He put the palms of his hands flat on his thighs and looked over at Odell, who sat straight and erect behind his desk, waiting. "So we've got three young women who disappeared without taking any of their belongings. Thought at first they were going to a party.

Then probably taken or detained against their will. You know what that sounds like."

Odell said, "Yep." He said it quietly, as if he didn't want the world to know, as if he could keep the world from knowing.

"It sounds like kidnapping" Balls continued, "which means we oughta alert the federal guys." He watched Odell's face. "The agent I'd feel most confident of and one that's really good is Larry Calvins. He's been with the bureau for fifteen or more years. Level headed. Not stuck on himself. Stationed in Raleigh and Rocky Mount."

"I've met him," Odell said. "I agree with you."

"You'll check with the sheriff? Let him know?"

Odell nodded.

"He'll come into town quietly," Balls said. "No need to advertise that we've got the FBI working with us on this."

I shifted a bit in my chair. Balls turned to me. "Go ahead," he said. "I know you can't wait to run your mouth."

"Playing devil's advocate," I said, "let's look at what we've got—"

"Whadda you mean *we*?" Balls said. "Where you get this Lindberg stuff of 'we'?" He sounded gruff, but he could barely conceal a grin.

"Okay," I said. "I'll start over. What *you've* got right now is one homicide, Thomas Findley . . ."

"And why you think he got done in? Huh?" Balls said.

"Yes, I know. It was probably because he said he was going to tell me what happened to those girls . . . or *the* girls. But we—excuse me—*you* don't know that they were kidnapped. It's still possible that they decided to leave the area . . . or maybe even that they were murdered. To assume they were kidnapped is connecting dots that might not be there."

Odell spoke up. "If it's human trafficking, and it likely is, then the feds are sure as hell gonna get involved."

I was quiet a moment. I remembered what Sam had said at the airport about her boyfriend's female worker who had

gone missing. "You are probably right on the human trafficking." Then I told them about the missing construction
worker. There was no real reason I hadn't mentioned it
earlier. Hadn't got around to it, and maybe I wasn't connecting the dots as much as I should have.

Odell wasn't through. "And one thing I haven't mentioned, Mr. Weaver, is that one of the executive directors of
this organization 'Stop Human Trafficking Now' has been to
me several times in the past few weeks suspecting that quite
a bit of human trafficking is going on now at the Outer
Banks. More than we would expect. The area is ripe for it—
what with many young people coming here for the summer,
hoping for jobs. Some of them give out of money, or get into
drugs, and first thing you know . . ."

I nodded, agreeing. Somewhat feebly, I said, "Well, as I
mentioned, I wanted to play devil's advocate."

"One other thing," Odell said, "is that your friend Linda
Shackleford is working on a series about human trafficking
here at the Outer Banks. So it's going to be in the news. Oh,
and this Friday night that Stop Human Trafficking outfit is
having a seminar, or public forum or something, here at the
courthouse."

Balls said to me, "Okay, you through running your
mouth?"

I nodded back at him.

"And speaking of connecting those dots," Balls said,
"let's take a look at them. First, we get this drowning in the
ocean of a young woman dressed in party clothes, who was
supposedly going to a party. Then we got two girls missing
after they announced they were going to a party. Maybe a
third one—that construction worker, and maybe more. Then
this Findley guy calls and says he can tell you what happened to the women, and he ends up dead. Executed. And he
works as a deckhand on various fishing boats—or maybe
party boats."

He tilted his chair back again on the two rear legs. Satisfied. "You don't have to be an expert at connecting dots to get to figuring that it's all linked together—and it seems like maybe these ladies are being carried away somewhere."

Balls stood. To Odell he said, "I'll go talk to Sheriff Albright about involving the FBI."

"Fine," Odell said. "I'll go with you."

I stood also.

Balls said, "Then you and me, Odell, may want to catch up with Duvall and Dorsey see whether they've run into anything with at the docks about Findley."

To me, Balls said, "And you can go downstairs and see your sweetie." He shook his head as if in serious disbelief. "What she can see in a dirty-neck newspaper guy like you beats me."

"My charming manner," I said. "And luck on my part."

Balls stood still, a serious expression of concern coming across his face. "Yeah, you got some luck all right. You're lucky you didn't get to that place behind Jockey's Ridge when the shooting started. You might not be with us today."

"Yes, I know." My voice was quiet.

I thought for a moment he might actually put his hand on my shoulder. "You take care of yourself," he said. Then the old Balls was there once again: "Okay, Odell, let's go talk to the sheriff."

Chapter Fifteen

Going downstairs, I went to the door of the Register of Deeds office. It was too early for lunch, but I was hoping to speak briefly to Elly. She was busy getting a document for a paralegal from one of the attorney's office. Elly glanced up at me and I mouthed that I'd be back at noon. With the slightest nod of her head, she affirmed my message. She continued engaging with the paralegal.

I could sense from Elly's expression that she wasn't too pleased with me. Probably because last night on the phone I had not told her about the homicide or my presence at the scene, which I'm sure Mabel or someone had told her about.

There was time for me to go upstairs to the coffee shop on Sir Walter Raleigh Street, get an espresso, and then also stop in and speak to Jamie, owner of Downtown Books. Distinguishable and exclusive aromas of both places always pleased me. First there was the heady scent of freshly brewed coffee, and then across the street at Downtown Books there was welcoming smell of new books.

I took my espresso outside to one of the tables along the narrow wooden walkway. The sun was out and the humidity down. Lovely day. A slight breeze came off the waterfront.

While I sat there enjoying the late morning and the espresso, a sheriff department's cruiser came from around the courthouse and headed down toward 64 with Odell driving.

Balls sat in the passenger seat. He was turned toward Odell and apparently talking. They were going to check with Duvall and Dorsey, see if they had any luck finding out anything about Findley's place or places of employment. Maybe they were checking into something else as well.

I thought about human trafficking; it was modern-day slave trading. There had to be money exchanging hands. Money was involved in virtually all crimes. "Follow the money" was a mantra used by most investigators. I thought about that. Maybe that's what we needed to concentrate on now.

A woman walked by me going into the coffee shop and she said good morning and I smiled and said good morning to her and what a nice day it was.

I finished the coffee and went down the outside steps to the street and across to Jamie's bookstore. She was behind the counter doing something on her laptop computer. She saw me and smiled.

"Those two books?" I said.

"Oh, yes, they're here," she said. From the side of the counter she produced the two books I had called her about: Paula McLain's *Love and Ruin*, a novel about Hemingway and Martha Gellhorn's marriage, his third wife; and then the other book was the memoir by A. E. Hotchner, a long-time friend and admirer of Hemingway, called *Hemingway in Love*. The memoir chronicled Hemingway's musings on his life and love of Hadley Richardson, his first wife, who was with him in Paris in the early 1920s. In one of my trips to Paris I walked up the hill to Contrescarpe where Hemingway and Hadley had their first apartment. There's a plaque on the building at No. 74 rue du Cardinal Lemoine commemorating the fact that the American writer lived there. Sort of paying homage.

It's always a pleasure visiting with Jamie. She's very supportive of writers—and readers too, of course.

After paying for the books, I took them out to my car

and then headed back to the courthouse. Lunchtime. Under-
standably, Elly was a little put out with me for not filling her
in last night on the phone about the homicide at Jockey's
Ridge. Finding out about it this morning at the courthouse—
and the fact that I was the first one on the scene—did not
register too well with her, I was sure. I'd have to do a bit of
diplomacy.

When I went into the courthouse, Elly was ready for
lunch. As always she looked fresh and pretty. She always reminded me of sunshine and fresh cotton. She wore light tan
slacks, fitted nicely, a soft pink collared blouse. He hair was
pinned up in the back, but one or two wispy strands of hair
graced her neck. Made me want to kiss the back of her neck.

"Ready?" she said. To Janet, one of her coworkers, she
said, "Lunch. Back in a bit."

"Have fun," Janet said with a lilt in her voice. The way
she said it, she tried to make it sound as if we were about to
engage in something naughty.

Elly was quiet as we left the courthouse.

"Ortega'z?" I said, referring to the Southwestern
restaurant a few doors down the street.

"Fine," she said as we walked.

I've been around long enough to know that when a
woman says "fine" that means that things aren't fine. Not at
all.

I figured best I dive right in. "Sorry I didn't tell you on
the phone last night about the homicide."

"Mabel filled me in this morning."

I opened the door to Ortega'z and held it for her to enter.
We were shown to a booth two from the front.

"I know it was a little—what?—embarrassing to learn
about it from Mabel when I should have mentioned it last
night." We were seated and she looked across at me. I
wanted to try to explain a bit more. "But I knew you were
busy with Martin and you'd just come in and all of that . . ."
My voice trailed off, waiting for her.

The young man who announced he would be our server, brought water and flatware. He said his name but I didn't catch it. As for anything else to drink we both told him water was all, at least for the time being. We both ordered one of their specialties: grilled chicken taco salads.

Elly arranged her flatware and appeared to be studying it. Then she said, "Of course I was surprised that first thing this morning Mabel started talking to me about the man who was killed, as if I knew all about it."

"Sorry about that."

"Maybe, as you said, it was a little embarrassing since you were involved and she thought . . ."

"I wasn't exactly *involved*," I said.

"Yes, you were." She leveled her eyes at me. But it wasn't with anger; her eyes registered more concern, worry, maybe a touch of sadness. "It's just, Harrison, that every time I begin to get used to the kind of work you do—writing about crime and all—just about the time I get used to it, something comes up and you get yourself in danger, real danger, where something could happen to you."

She reached one hand across the table and touched my wrist. "I don't want to lose you." There was a glistening in her eyes.

"Oh, Elly," I said, "I'm not going to let anything happen to me."

"Suppose you had gotten there a little earlier . . . when the killer was there?"

There was nothing I could really say. So I kept quiet. She stared again at her flatware, and with one slender finger moved the fork back and forth. Her nails were clear and pretty. I knew what she was thinking—about losing me.

We had both suffered losses. Her husband had died after they had been married only two years and she was pregnant with Martin. It was now more than four years ago my wife, Keely, also a musician, a really good jazz vocalist, had slipped deeper and deeper into depression, a depth where no one could reach her, died of an overdose of pills. She didn't just *die*: she committed suicide, a haunting tragedy I wrestled with in a state of sad bewilderment for months and months.

The server brought our food and said, "Enjoy." He asked if there was anything else we needed and we said we were good. In a few minutes he refilled our water glasses.

In what was probably an empty gesture, I promised Elly again I would be careful and that I didn't think I had been in any danger going to meet that young man on the south side of Jockey's Ridge. That last part was a lie, of course. I think we were both aware of that.

After a while she said, "Do you think you might still be in danger from that person, that killer? I mean suppose he thinks that you do know something. That the man who was killed told you more than he did over phone?" Obviously, Mabel had filled Elly in with all the details, details I didn't know Mabel knew. But I should have been aware that nothing happens at the courthouse that Mabel doesn't know about, in detail.

"Oh, I think *they*, the mean guys, monitored his phone call to me—how else would they have known where he was going to meet me?—and if they did monitor the call, they'd know that he didn't and wouldn't tell me anything over the phone."

She picked at her taco salad. I was half through with mine. She did eat another piece of the grilled chicken, and then she looked up at me: "Do you really think this involves human trafficking?"

"That's what Deputy Wright and Agent Twiddy think." I took another big bite of the taco salad, mixing in some of the salsa and sour cream. "I go along with them."

"I mean, what do they do with the women? And I guess it's all or mostly women?"

"It is," I said. "They sell them or get them involved in prostitution. Sometimes labor, working for somebody with little or no pay or little or no chance of getting away."

"Harrison, that's like slavery." She had two frown lines between her eyebrows. "That is the same as slavery."

I nodded. "Yes, it is."

When the waiter brought the check, he asked Elly if she'd like a little box to take the remains of her salad with her. She smiled and thanked him and said it was good but that she didn't want to take the leftover with her.

We walked slowly in the sunshine back toward the courthouse. Elly said, "You've got a busy week, haven't you? I mean with playing Wednesday and flying Thursday morning." She playfully nudged me with her elbow. "And getting involved in murder investigations."

Okay, she was feeling better. That was good.

She added, "And, oh yes, you're also a writer. Correct? You've got to squeeze in some actual writing time in there, too."

We both chuckled and slowed our walk even more. "Actually, the job Wednesday will be one of the last ones for the summer, I believe." I played bass with the Jim Watson Jazz Combo two or three times a month. Mostly in the summer. Wednesday we would be playing from one p.m. to three p.m. at the deck at Scarborough Faire, outside Bill Rickman's Island Bookstore, one of three that he owned. And, yes, there was another flying lesson scheduled for Thursday morning. Writing to be done, too.

We stepped up on the porch of the courthouse. "I'd better get on to work," Elly said, "and I thank you so much for lunch."

"Thursday night?" I said.

"Yes, that would be very nice."

"We'll go out to eat." I lowered my voice, and did a corny version of trying to appear wicked and seductive. "Then maybe swing by my house for a bit?"

She raised one eyebrow, but there was a smile there. "Maybe," she said. Then she became serious, but there was no anger there any longer. "In the meantime, please try to stay out of trouble . . . and don't put yourself in danger."

"Promise," I said.

We parted and I headed toward my car. I would, indeed, try to avoid any danger—and stay out of trouble—but there were a couple of things I wanted to follow up on.

Chapter Sixteen

When I got in my house, the first thing I did after speaking to Janey was to go to the phone, check for messages—there were none—and then call Dee to see how she was doing and if funeral arrangements had been made for Marisa.

She answered her cell phone on the third ring. I could tell from her breathing she had rushed to the phone. Probably cleaning at someone's house. "Hope I'm not interrupting you," I said, "but I'm just checking with you to see how you are doing."

She said she was fine, and that she had picked up two more houses to clean. Although I was a bit unclear on what she said further, I gathered that at least one of these had been a customer of Marisa's.

Before I could get around to asking about the funeral arrangements, she said, "Funeral Saturday for Marisa. Ten o'clock." She named the funeral home where Marisa's body had been taken initially.

"I'll hope to be there," I said.

"*Gracias.*"

Trying to make it sound as casual as possible, I asked if Dee had any new information as to where that party was supposed to be that Marisa was attending.

"No," she said. "*Nada.*"

"Me either." I said I'd see her Saturday at the service.

I sat there in my little chair by the phone. Then after a few minutes I called Chief Deputy Odell Wright. I started to call him at the sheriff's office, through the dispatcher, but decided to try him on his cell, since I now had the number he had given me quite willingly. He answered right away.

"Don't want to pester you, Odell, but checking, if you don't mind, on how it went this afternoon with you and Balls."

"You're not pestering. Almost wish something would get me really pestered instead of just being frustrated." He sighed. "We didn't have much luck at the marinas. A few people recognized the picture of Findley and said he'd worked on the boats from time to time, but no one knew where he'd gone."

I made some sort of comment, commiserating.

"After hanging around the marinas," Odell said, "we went up to Southern Shores to Claire's restaurant, where the two women worked. We tried to talk with a couple of her co-workers, but they held back and obviously didn't much wanna talk with us." He shook his head. "Balls said we intimidated them." A slight pause. "He said—and this is the truth—that you might have better luck talking to them, the coworkers. I said something about how you were not official, or something like that, and he said—his exact words—'Ain't no way to keep him quiet and out of it.'" Now there was a genuine chuckle. "No matter how he runs his mouth, he really has a lot of respect for you."

"And I for him," I said. "He's a piece of work."

Then Odell spoke more quietly. "Incidentally, the sheriff doesn't want to bring in the FBI yet. He doesn't want them to take over. I feel he may change his mind, though." He paused, then said, "Sheriff's debating whether to have a press conference maybe tomorrow or Wednesday. He's getting media calls."

I was silent a moment. "A press conference," I mumbled, a hint of doubt tingeing my tone. "What would he be prepared to tell them? I mean, would the business of human trafficking come up? The two—and maybe three—missing young women? Or would the conference center only on the homicide of Findley?"

I was silent for two or three seconds, and shook my head with concern. Odell waited for me to continue. I said, "Would there be a chance that speculation comes up linking all three events—the missing women, the drowning, and the homicide? It could, and I'm not sure how the sheriff would want to handle that. Hell," I said, "I'm not even sure I can get my head around all of that, making a linkage. But he'd need to be prepared as to how much he'd want to speculate."

Now it was Odell's turn to pause a bit, apparently mulling over what I had said. "Let me talk with him. See how far he'd be prepared to go." I heard him sigh. "Maybe he's thinking about appealing to the public. You know, enlist support for the missing persons. I don't know. I'll discuss it with him."

That was about the end of our conversation, with assurance from Odell that he or Mabel would let me know if and when there would be a press conference. I stood up from the chair by the phone and stretched my back.

My parakeet muttered in the background, as if she were talking to herself. She does that sometimes before she takes a nap.

The afternoon sun was getting lower in the southwest. I didn't feel like cooking anything for supper. Wasn't all that hungry. Then I got a half-crooked smile on my face. Might mosey over to Claire's for light dinner. Chat with the people there if Balls thinks I can glean something from them that he and Odell were not able to.

I thought, too, about whether I needed to talk with anyone else that I knew Marisa had worked for. Only ones I could recall was the couple living near Barbara and Dwight Reid. Their neighbor had made a trip up to Maine and might be back now. Well, I'd check later.

Admittedly without a whole lot of enthusiasm, I prepared to drive up to Claire's in Southern Shores. First, I washed my face and cleaned up a bit; put a few more seeds in Janey's dish. I started to lift up the bass and play, but gave a big sigh, giving up that idea, and went down the outside stairs to the carport.

In the side yard, I did a quick check to make sure the canvas covered my boat properly. The eighteen-foot Ranger was trailered, and my rusty old Jeep I used to tow the boat was parked in front of the boat. I vowed to go out in the sound with the boat in the next few days. Needed to run it.

After my cursory inspection of the boat and Jeep, I got in my Outback, started the engine and headed up to Claire's, where I would try to be charming.

Actually, when I made my left turn off the Duck Road just beyond the Beach Road and parked in front of Claire's and went inside, I grinned really big. The smile wasn't forced, either, because the hostess turned out to be friend Terri, whom I had known for about three years when she had worked at other restaurants at the Outer Banks.

She hugged me in greeting. Lots of hugs are exchanged at the Outer Banks. "Well, well," she said, "what a great pleasure it is to have you grace us with your presence." Terri is probably late forties, early fifties, rather tall, face touched by a lifetime of beach sun; her hair, with a few strands of gray, pulled back in an unruly ponytail. She's got a great and genuine smile.

"Yes, and good to see you too, Terri." We stood there grinning at each other. "I might be accused of stalking you from one restaurant to the other."

"Oh, I've been here since the beginning of summer," she said. "It's that you haven't been around."

"I've been looking for you. Trying one restaurant after the other."

She leaned forward to speak more softly. "You're full of crap, you know."

"Yes, but charming. Right?"

"Dinner?" she said. "Or'd you just come to flirt with me?"

"Mostly to flirt with you but since I'm here, and you'll be busy, I might as well eat something . . . something light."

"Just you?" She picked up a menu. "Follow me," she said.

"Gladly."

She tossed a smile back over her shoulder at me as I followed her to a booth about midway down against the wall on the ocean side. "Janika will be your server." She laid the menu on the table and stood there a moment, a quick glance toward the hostess stand at the front, and then leaned forward with one hand on the edge of the table. "What are you working on?" she said quietly.

I flipped open the menu and pretended to be as innocent as all get-out. "Oh, what makes you think I'm working on anything?"

"'Cause I know you." Another glance toward the front, then back at me. "Besides, two officers were in here earlier today. I'm sure you know both of them. They were asking about the two workers here who have disappeared. And then you come in this evening. Not a coincidence." She cocked her head at me, that grin there.

"I was wondering if maybe there was someone they became real friendly with here and maybe, you know, decided to take off." I pretended to take an interest in the menu.

Two women and a man came in from the front, approaching the hostess stand.

"I'll try to get back with you," Terri said, and hurried up front to greet the trio.

A young waitress came to my booth. She said her name and I think it was Janika, the name Terri had mentioned as my server. She was young, early twenties maybe, very trim, almost tiny, a pretty face with large eyes. Her light brown hair was shoulder-length but pulled back with a clip. She had that delightful accent signaling she was probably from somewhere in Russia. She smiled a little shyly, and put a tall glass of water on my table, along with a white cloth napkin wrapped around flatware.

Janika asked if I would like something else besides water to drink. I told her water was fine. "I'll give you a minute to decide the menu," she said, and then added, almost apologetically, "Unless you want to place your order now."

"Give me a minute or two," I said, and said it as pleasantly as possible. A smile, too. Wanted her to know I was friendly. It helped, I hoped, that she had seen me chatting with Terri.

Giving the menu a cursory scan, I settled on a shrimp and light pasta dish. In a couple of minutes, Janika came to me again. Maybe she did that with all customers, but it seemed to me she approached with wariness, as if maybe she didn't want to intrude, or even that the customer might pose a danger of some unidentified nature.

I placed my order, again with a smile, and I asked her where she was from. She mentioned a town she said was south of Moscow but I didn't know it and wasn't sure I understood. I said welcome and that I hoped she liked it here, and then I asked how long she had been here and she said since the spring and she shifted from one foot to the other, obviously wanting to spring away from talking to me, and go place my order.

No question about it; I would have better luck talking with Terri than I would with Janika.

My food came quickly, and Janika wasted no time hanging around my table. She said, "Enjoy," and scurried back to her station.

The meal was good. A light, creamy sauce graced the pasta and the shrimp were fat and succulent.

Janika came back one time to refill my water glass and she asked if I needed anything else. She appeared a bit more relaxed.

As I was finishing, and as there was a break in traffic up front, Terri came briefly to my booth. "Maybe we can talk a bit before you leave." She grinned, "You can always hang around up front as if you're hitting on me."

"Sounds like a plan," I said, taking a bite of the last shrimp.

I signaled quite discreetly for Janika to bring me my check. She approached and appeared more comfortable since I obviously was getting ready to leave. I thanked her and asked her if she had to return home soon. With a broad smile, she said she would leave at the end of the month. "I have to get back to school," she said.

"Oh, where?"

Then proudly: "University of Moscow. My last year. I be graduated in May."

"Congratulations," I said.

Still smiling, she said, "Business administration."

I settled the bill and left her a nice tip and made my way up front, standing to one side while Terri dealt with a young couple and got them seated.

"Meal okay?" she said when she returned.

"Fine," I said. "Very good," and I told her what I had. She said it was one of her favorite dishes.

With her elbows resting on the hostess stand, she spoke softly to me. "Okay, I know you want to know what I may know about what might have happened to Olga and Masha." I stood close to the stand. She leaned toward me. "I wish I knew. They were here and seemed happy and content, and then they were gone. They had been talking about how much they enjoyed being here at the Outer Banks. Just the same, I think they were looking forward to going home at the end of the summer." She shook her head. "Here one day, gone the next. No word at all."

"Did they make any special friends here at the restaurant?"

"No, not really. Some of the young guys would try flirting with them. They were friendly, but didn't, you know, set-tle on any of the guys."

"They were supposed to be going to a party that night. You know anything about that?"

"Not a thing."

A foursome came in the front door, talking animatedly to each other. I stepped back and moved toward a display case. Terri took care of them and a minute or so later came back to the hostess stand. Elbows again resting on the top.

"Oh, there was one person," she said, "who spent time talking with Masha and Olga. But this was an older woman, almost grandmotherly, and both of the girls seemed to like her a lot and be comfortable with her. She usually came for a late lunch when we aren't too busy and the servers have a bit more freedom."

Terri stood straighter and spoke to two men who were leaving. "I hope you enjoyed. Please come back." They said it was very good and they would be back.

Terri turned to me. "This woman came in at least twice a week for a good month or more. Sometimes three times a week. The girls liked her. That was obvious. And they spent a lot of time talking with her. One or the other would always be her server, but the other one would join in usually and talk with her. I felt like almost they confided in her." With a short laugh, she said, "Plus she was very generous—very gener-ous—with her tips."

I watched Terri's face. "Do you know her name?"

She shrugged. "Well, I would have if she'd paid with a credit card. But she always—always—paid cash." A little twitch of her shoulders. "Most people pay with a credit card. Oh, cash once in a while. But not every time."

My eyes were downcast. I rubbed a finger along the ledge of the hostess stand. Then I looked up at Terri. "Maybe the two young women might have told this woman where the party was that they were supposed to be attending."

"Yes, that's possible."

"When was the last time you saw this lady?"

Terri took a breath, ready to speak, but then an expression of perplexity clouded her face. "That's curious," she said. "Now that you asked, I realize she hasn't been back since Olga and Masha disappeared. I haven't seen her for about a week at least."

"Yes, that is curious," I said softly.

Chapter Seventeen

Terri smiled a "Welcome to Claire's" greeting to a man and woman who entered with a pre-teenage girl. All three of the new arrivals were badly sunburned. Too long on the beach today. Undoubtedly not from the Outer Banks; here on vacation.

No sooner had Terri seated them than others began arriving. Time for me to leave. As Terri returned quickly to her station, I met her halfway and slipped her one of my cards. "Call me if that woman returns."

She nodded. "Will do." Then more audibly, "Come back to see us, sweetie." In addition to frequent hugs, there're a lot of "sweeties," "sugars" and "honeys" spoken at the Outer Banks.

I got in my car, started the engine, and drove out the backside of the small shopping area onto Duck Road. It would be easier at the intersection to make my left turn and head south along Beach Road. I wanted to park at the unloading area beyond Hilton Garden Inn and walk up the overlook to absorb the ocean and think. Viewing the ocean, breathing in the air off the surf was the best place in the world to let your thoughts spread out so you could get a better handle on them.

As I've known over the years, the ocean becomes something of a sanctuary for me, my place of reverence. My church.

And these barrier islands, these Outer Banks that stretch a hundred miles down the coast, are conducive for that kind of reverence. From the air, and on a map, they appear fragile. But though winds and surf and storms may change them from time to time, reshape them a bit, they remain. They are sinewy and tough. They remain.

I spent several minutes there leaning against the railing and watching the surf and looking out forever at the ocean. Several stiff-legged sandpipers skirted up and down the beach, managing to stay inches away from the incoming surf. The sun was low behind me and the ocean changed colors as the light changed.

I heard or felt someone coming up the wooden walkway. Half-turning, I nodded a greeting to an elderly man and two women of about the same age. They spoke and commented on what a lovely early evening it was, and I agreed, and prepared to leave the view to them.

Paying my respects to the ocean—to its power and vastness—always made me feel better and I felt good driving to my house as twilight approached.

Tuesday morning I was up at a reasonable hour, and after coffee and a bite to eat, I got down to the writing. Working on an article for Rose, my editor, and running a little behind. Somewhat surprisingly, I was going good when the phone rang. I muttered an expletive and started not to answer it because I was in the middle of a paragraph that I liked; but the old reporter's instinct kicked in and I couldn't let a phone go unanswered.

Checking the caller ID, it was listed as D. Reid and I was puzzled with that. It rang again, and then I remembered that was the name of the couple I talked with about Marisa, so I answered before voice mail engaged.

Barbara Reid, the wife, said she hoped she wasn't interrupting me but that I had expressed an interest in talking to her neighbors about Marisa—the brother and sister who had been in Maine. "They're back now," she said. "They've maybe been back two days or more and it occurred to me you might want to check with them. I know you talked to some other people who Marisa worked for, but I figured that maybe . . ."

"That's very thoughtful of you," I said when she paused enough for me to interject. "Yes, I would like to chat with them a bit. Maybe I can drift over there later this morning." Then to a question from her, I said, "No, no real luck on where that party was she was attending."

After a few more exchanges and after agreeing with her that it was a shame what happened to the young lady, I thanked her again and we ended the conversation.

Maybe subconsciously I was looking for an excuse to get away from the writing for a while, so I figured maybe I'd drive up to Kitty Hawk Landing and drift in to see the brother and sister for whom Marisa worked. I checked my notes to make sure of their names: Basil and Eunice Cleave. I didn't know how long they'd been in Maine, but probably not long, from the way Barbara spoke about them. And I was at a place in my writing where I knew what was coming next. I agreed with Hemingway's advice to only stop writing when you knew what comes next. Makes it easier to restart.

I stirred around my house for a while, letting time pass; didn't want to arrive too early at the home of Basil and Eunice Cleave. Late morning would be civilized.

By close to eleven, I drove up the Bypass to Woods Road, made my left and wended my way to Kitty Hawk Landing. I passed the Reid's house and went up a few more houses to the large, two-story white and rust-colored house that belonged to Basil and Eunice Cleave.

I parked in the paved circular driveway behind a fairly new pickup truck. At the side of the large house, a door of the two-car garage was open and I could see the dark blue rear of what I figured was a Buick or Lincoln. Maybe a Cadillac.

Cutting the engine on my Subaru, I swung my legs out and stood for a moment before shutting the car door. I could see toward the canal in the back of the house and had a fairly good view of that nice boat that the Cleaves owned. A guy in knee-length shorts and sleeveless T-shirt was on the stern of the boat; he appeared to be working on the engine. He glanced up at me and then went back to work. He held a wrench of some kind in one hand.

I started to walk toward the boat when a tall man came out of the garage. It had to be Basil Cleave. He was dressed immaculately: sharply creased khaki slacks, a Ralph Lauren boldly striped shirt with the Polo emblem where normally a breast pocket would be. He had longish silver hair, neatly brushed and swept back at the sides.

He approached me and I put out may hand and introduced myself. "Oh, yes," he said. "Barbara Reid said you might stop by, inquiring about poor Marisa. I'm Basil Cleave."

"Good to meet you," I said. "Yes, that's why I stopped by. Hope you don't mind." I nodded toward the boat. "I was admiring your boat. A real beauty."

"Very proud of it," he said. "And that's my captain, or first mate, and general maintenance chief tuning up the engine to get it running like a purring cat. His name is Clete."

Clete glanced from his work, raised the wrench as a greeting. He smiled but the smile didn't reach his eyes.

"The boat sleeps eight. We've taken her out on a number of overnight trips. Drove it up to Maine once." He chuckled. "At least Capt'n Clete drove us up to Maine in it."

We stood there a moment admiring the boat, while Clete continued to monkey with the engine. We had moved to within about thirty feet of the docked boat.

Basil said, "I know you are interested in . . . in the tragedy about Marisa. Wish I could help you on that. Barbara said you were asking about where she was supposed to be going to a party that night." He shook his head. "She didn't confide in us about her personal life, and I'm not sure I could have understood her if she did." A sort of knowing smile as if he and I were in on something. "But I got the impression, probably from her general demeanor, that maybe she went to quite a few parties."

I nodded but didn't say anything.

There in the back yard near the canal, I got a good view of the rear of his elegant home. A rear deck ran most of the length of the house. The glass storm door opened and a woman came out on the deck. She appeared to be maybe a couple of years older than Basil. She was not turned out quite as elegantly as Basil. She wore loose-fitting slacks and a bulky, short-sleeved sweatshirt. Her gray hair was pulled back and secured, mostly. A suburban, vaguely harried, grandmother type. Much like Barbara Reid.

He called to her. "Eunice, this is Mr. Weaver. He's the one asking about poor Marisa." To me he said, "That's my sister."

Eunice acknowledged me with a faint smile that disappeared quickly. "Wish we could help," she said. "A sad thing."

I hadn't said anything to her about what I was asking about. Perhaps Barbara Reid had filled her in as well.

Eunice smiled a goodbye at me, turned and went back in the house.

It was obvious I was not going to get any more here than I had at the other places where Marisa had worked. She didn't confide in anyone about the location of the party she planned to attend . . . and maybe with those other two young women who disappeared.

A few more pleasantries with the highly polished Basil Cleave, and I prepared to leave. I yelled a good-to-meet-you at Clete. He managed a short wave but didn't look up from the engine.

That is, he didn't look up from the engine until I was in my car with the motor running and ready to back out of the driveway. He stared at me a moment; then once again trained his attention on the engine.

I left and headed home once again.

When I got home, the message light on my answering machine was blinking. I pushed the play button. It was Chief Deputy Odell Wright. "Give me a ring when you get a minute."

I sat in the little chair by the phone and called the sheriff's office. After a couple of clicks I got Odell.

"Thought I'd give you a heads up," he said. "The sheriff has decided to go ahead with a press conference—probably. But only after he talks with the FBI guy."

"FBI? I thought he'd given up on that idea."

"Changed his mind."

There was a long pause, and I waited, sensing that Odell had something else to say. I thought maybe I could jump start him a bit, so I said, "What prompted this change? About bringing in the Feds?"

Odell cleared his throat and then spoke very softly. "I haven't been instructed not to say anything—but there's another body. Another young woman."

I'm not sure what I said next. Probably an expletive, or something similar. But I did manage to say, "Details?"

He continued quietly. "Not much yet. Caucasian female, late twenties probably. Found off the highway over in Mann's Harbor." Then he added, "Nude. Completely nude."

"ID? Or a Jane Doe."

"A Jane Doe right now."

"When was this, Odell? I mean when was she found?"

"Early this morning. A motorist stopped when he thought he saw the lower part of a human leg."

I'll admit I was a tad miffed that I didn't know about

this earlier—while instead I was thinking about chasing what
turned out to be a dead-end with Basil Cleave and his sister.
But after all, there was no reason to alert me. I have to re-
mind myself of that quite often. I'm not part of the investigative team, even though I do manage to insinuate myself
into what's going on quite frequently.

To Odell, I said, "How was she killed? And when?"

"Dr. Willis did a prelim. No obvious trauma to the body.
Know more about the cause of death from Greenville when
they do a complete. For now, the body's here locally. As to
when, probably last night. A few hours before she was
found. Not a whole lot of effort to conceal her. Just sort of
dumped."

I said, "What about Balls . . . Agent Twiddy . . . is he involved?"

"He couldn't break free today. Be down in the morning.
Agent Twiddy wants to take a look. Right now we're trying
to get an ID. No luck yet."

Tomorrow morning I wanted to be there when Balls
arrived. Had that jazz job with Jim Watson at one o'clock up
at Duck, but I'd still have time to poke my nose into this
latest, at any rate.

Odell spoke again, "I'm gonna have to sign off but a
curious thing that might be a clue to the ID, is that her fore-
arms and hands were really tanned and her hands were like
she did hard outdoor type work."

I didn't say anything, but like a light bulb went off in
my head I remembered what Sam said at the airport after my
lesson Sunday—that a female construction worker for her
boyfriend had gone missing.

Chapter Eighteen

Before I let Odell sign off, I said, "Now this is a long shot, Odell. I'll be the first to admit that, but my flight instructor—Samantha Inez Davis, or Sam as she's called—said her boyfriend, Robert-something, who has a construction company, well one of his workers—a young woman who was a project manager—has gone missing. Now if this body that was discovered . . ."

Odell broke in. "Certainly worth checking into. Is she at the Manteo airport?"

"Yes."

"I'll check it out. Thanks."

"I'll give her a ring. Tell her you may drop by. Okay?"

"Sure."

I called the airport and got Sam right away. I told her Deputy Odell Wright might stop by, get a bit more information from her—like how to get in touch with Robert and talk with him about his worker who has gone missing. I didn't tell her about the body.

She said she knew Odell, and had met the worker for Robert, and that he was, indeed, worried about her. The woman wasn't the type who would leave without saying anything.

I hung up, and not a minute later, the phone rang and I picked it up quickly, figuring it was Sam or Odell calling back with another question or comment. I didn't even bother to check caller ID.

The voice on the other end of the line was muffled, obviously disguised. It was low and guttural, like talking through a mechanical device. But the message was clear and chilling:

"Stop looking into what happened to those girls or you'll end up like Findley."

I managed to stammer, "Who is . . . ?"

But the line went dead.

I gripped the handset tightly and stared at the ID. It said caller unknown and had a number I didn't recognize.

That's not the kind of call anyone wants to receive. And I didn't like it. It was frightening. I don't mind saying that. Findley, of course, was the young man at the beach area I came to meet—and he had three bullet holes in him. No, you don't want to end up like Findley.

Obviously someone was worried. Someone including me. We must be getting close. That can be good in an investigation. But it can also be deadly.

Deadly I didn't want.

I realized I had stood, still holding the handset. I put it down gingerly in the cradle as if I wanted to be careful with it. Then I strode across the living room. Janey chirped and I ignored her. I went back to the phone and stared at it. I picked it up and called Balls on his cell. I needed to tell him.

"Yeah?" he said. "Whadda you want? Don't you know I'm busy?"

"Balls," I said. "I need to tell you something."

From the tone and timbre of my voice he knew something serious was up. He immediately mellowed. "Yeah? What's wrong?"

I told him about the call and repeated the message word-for-word.

"Shit," he said. "That's not good."

"I know. I don't think it's good either."

"You've poked a stick in someone's hornet's nest. What have you been doing?"

"Well, very little, actually. I went to Clare's and chatted a bit there and I've followed up on where Marisa, that drowned girl, worked . . . and that's about it. Except for that call from Thomas Findley to meet him at that beach area. And that was a call he initiated. Not me." I swallowed audibly. "And you know how he ended up."

Balls was quiet a moment. "You're home now." It was a statement; not a question. "Stay there. Keep everything locked tight. Keep that little handgun of yours handy . . . and the phone. Tomorrow morning I'll be coming to the court-house early. I'll pick you up first. Seven-thirty or so."

"I'll be ready," I said.

"Alert Odell. And, damnit, call Odell or 911 if any-thing—anything at all—comes up in the meantime."

After we ended the call, I immediately called Odell and gave him the same information I'd given Balls. Odell said, "I think you better stick pretty close."

I intended to. Then I thought about Elly and her son Martin. It would be wise to stay away from her for the time being. Safer for her, too. I decided not to tell her anything about the call. No sense in alarming her further than she usually was when I managed to get myself involved in some-thing. Seems I've got a real knack for it.

Not sure what happened to the time that afternoon, but it went fast. I called Elly before she got off work. We talked a while and agreed I'd stay home tonight and probably see her Wednesday evening over at her house. She said for me to call her before I went to bed.

I ate a light supper early and then practiced the bass a short while. When I finished, I put the black canvas cover on it so I'd be ready to haul it to the car tomorrow and drive up to Duck. Be ready to play a few minutes before one.

Twice I went out on the deck and breathed in the even-ing air, drank in the sky and the early stars. When I went back in, I locked the sliding glass door and secured it doubly with the metal rod.

Putting my revolver on the bedside table, I went to bed early and read a while before turning off the light. I didn't think I'd go to sleep right away, but I did, and I didn't wake up until shortly before six in the morning. Got up and took a shower and sat out on the deck drinking coffee and waiting for Balls. I thought about the threatening call. Couldn't help it. But it didn't seem real. Hard to believe. Like something out of a B-grade movie.

Yet, it was real. And I knew I'd better treat it that way.

Shortly before seven-thirty, Balls' vintage Thunderbird came into view turning into my cul-de-sac. The low rumble of its engine sounding comfortable and familiar. He swung around deftly and backed into my driveway.

"Be right there," I called. Coming back from the deck, I locked the sliding glass door, spoke to Janey, put the night latch on the kitchen door and went quickly down the outside steps.

Balls nodded as I squeezed into the front seat. "Any more death threats overnight?"

"Quiet night," I said.

"Where's your handgun?"

"Bedside table."

He made sort of a dismissive humpf sound.

"I figured you'd have that big old Glock with you. Plenty of protection."

He shook his head and we drove out of the cul-de-sac and headed for the Bypass and south toward Manteo. "Got a few details from Odell on that woman's body. Get more when we get to the courthouse."

"ID on her yet?"

"I think so. Odell followed up on something yesterday."

I wondered whether that long shot I'd mentioned to Odell had paid off. We'd find out.

Balls was quiet for several minutes. The traffic was a bit

frustrating. He wasn't pushing it too much and it was fairly early. He drove mostly on the inside lane, passing a few cars with drivers deciding about breakfast. The sun was out and we put down the visors.

At Whalebone junction we swung west and the sun was not so much in our eyes. We crossed the high-rise bridge over Roanoke Sound, skirted Pirate's Cove and the marsh-land, took the right turn onto the Manteo road and a short time later parked at one of the reserved spots on the Budleigh Street side of the courthouse.

Upstairs we met Odell in the hallway. "Let's step into the sheriff's office," he said.

The door was partly open. Mabel exited and smiled a greeting at us as we entered. Sheriff Albright motioned to the two chairs in front of his desk. I started to stand but Odell insisted I take one of the chairs and he stood near the edge of Albright's desk.

The sheriff said, "Won't keep you all but a minute or two. Chief Deputy Wright wants to go over some things with you. First off, though, I wanted to let you know that I've decided two things. First, I've gone ahead and alerted FBI Agent Larry Calvins and asked him to come here and give us a hand. He'll be here this morning by ten o'clock. And, two, I've decided to honor the requests of some reporters and have a press conference at ten o'clock tomorrow morning. We've got two homicides, two young women missing—not to mention that suspicious drowning."

Balls cleared his throat. "I know Calvins. He's a good man." He leaned forward. "Sir, are you prepared to make a link with these events tomorrow at the press conference? I mean, the missing women, the homicides . . ."

"Well, no, Agent Twiddy, I hope we can keep it mainly to this latest homicide and the one over at Nags Head, that Findley man."

Balls spoke again. "If you don't mind me saying, we need to be prepared with an answer if some reporter does ask if there's a connection with the homicides and with the missing women."

"I don't think we know," Albright said.

Balls shrugged. "That's our answer if the question comes up."

Odell said, "If the missing women are asked about—and I'm sure some of the reporters know there was a report here at the department about them missing—Sheriff Albright has mentioned that we might consider asking that the reporters appeal to the public to report anything that might help us . . . like the party they were supposed to be attending. Anything at all."

Balls nodded, apparently satisfied.

Sheriff Albright looked at me. "Understand you got a threatening call yesterday. We want you to be careful."

"Yes, sir, I will."

Albright said. "Stay close to the big guy there," inclining his head toward Balls.

Then Albright said, "I think Odell wants to take the two of you to the room next door and fill you in on the preliminaries about the body found yesterday."

We left the sheriff's office. Next door was actually Mabel's small office, the homiest and the most comfortable in the department. She had a glowing lamp on her desk, along with pictures on the walls. Seascapes mostly, and on her desk were pictures of her two nieces and her nephew. Divorced decades earlier, Mabel was childless but had practically raised her sister's three children.

It was the windowless interrogation room next to Mabel's office that Balls, Odell and I entered. Odell took the seat on the far side of the table and Balls and I sat in metal chairs facing him.

Odell spoke to me. "Your long-shot paid off. We got an ID on that woman. I spoke to your flight instructor and she gave me the name of her boyfriend—Robert Stoddard. He came with me to the funeral home and did a positive. She's

Micki Mitchell." He glanced at his hands. "At least she *was* Micki Mitchell."

Balls said, "Long-shot? From Weave?"

"Yep," Odell said, and then he related to Balls what I had suggested yesterday as a remote possibility.

Nodding toward me, Balls said, "Well, he can be of use from time to time."

"Thanks."

"Where's the body now?" Balls asked.

"She's already over in Greenville. We should have— hope to have—a report from them by early tomorrow morning." Odell handed Balls a folder he had had with him when we were in the sheriff's office. "Pictures of the body at the scene."

Several eight-by-ten photos were in the folder. Balls studied them one at a time. I glanced at a couple of them. The nude woman was obviously dumped a few yards off the highway. Very little effort was made to conceal her.

"No known cause of death yet?" Balls asked.

"A prelim by Dr. Willis. He figured it was most likely an overdose. He did see needle marks on her body. Several of them." Odell raised an eyebrow. "One needle mark on her back."

Balls cocked his head. "Strange, huh? She didn't do that to herself."

Odell said, "And both that flight instructor, Sam, and her boyfriend said Micki was not a drug user. That she was afraid of drugs."

"Also, Willis wasn't sure about rape, but he was sure she'd been very active sexually. Maybe with multiple partners."

Neither Balls or I said anything.

Odell took the folder of pictures back from Balls. With the folder to one side, Odell trained his eyes at Balls and said, "From talking with Stoddard, her former boss, and with everything else going on, my theory is that she was abducted or tricked into going with someone, held several days some-where, shot full of dope, and maybe getting ready to be sold when they—the person or persons—who held her over-did it with the narcotics. And the body was taken out and dumped."

Balls said, "You're talking about kidnapping."

"Yep."

"That gives the Feds a reason to be here."

They talked on for several minutes, tossing out different theories, shooting some down, pursuing others. I glanced at my watch. Getting close to ten o'clock. Then suddenly it dawned on me: I had a job playing the bass with Jim Watson at one and I didn't have my car.

"Jeeze," I said during a brief break in their conversation. "I just realized I had to get home before noon, get my bass, go play up at Duck, Scarborough Faire."

Odell raised an eyebrow.

"He came with me," Balls said.

"Oh," Odell said. "I can probably get Deputy Dorsey to run you back home. Let me check." He got up and left the room.

"Sorry," I said. "I should have thought about that."

I thought Balls would make some smart-alecky remark. But he surprised me. "Maybe best you were with me, and then be with one of the deputies—for the time being anyway."

Odell reentered the room. "Dorsey'll take you a little after ten. He'll come up and get you."

Balls said, "If Dorsey can spare the time, and you maybe got something for him to do up at Duck, it wouldn't be bad for him to hang around while Hot Shot here is playing his cello or whatever the hell that big thing is. You know, sort of be a presence there."

"Good idea," Odell said. "I'll let him know."

Then we heard talking out in the hallway. Mabel was greeting someone. Probably FBI Agent Larry Calvins. Well, I did have a few more minutes before I had to leave.

I wanted to meet him.

Chapter Nineteen

In a moment or two the door opened and Sheriff Albright appeared with FBI Agent Larry Calvins.

Calvins was tall. Maybe a trim, athletic six-one or so. But another thing I noticed immediately was that he wore a dress shirt and tie. Ties were a rarity at the Outer Banks, even more rare than in the rest of the nation. Calvins' hair was neatly cut and parted. His eyebrows were heavy, and they emphasized the intensity of his gaze when he bore his sight toward you. You felt he was really looking at you.

Albright started the introductions. Calvins spoke up and extended his hand. "Good to see you again, Ballsford."

It was probably one of the few times I'd ever heard anyone speak to Balls using his full middle name.

Calvins shook my hand and cocked his head inquisitively. "And you're with . . ."

Balls spoke up. "Weaver here is not with anyone . . . except sort of with us. He's involved with what's going on because of a couple of things." Balls did a quick bob of his head. "I'll explain it to you—but he's got to go in a minute anyway." Balls gave me a look.

"Yes, I'll be leaving shortly," I said.

Balls said, "It's okay to talk around him. He's a writer but knows when to keep his mouth shut."

I moved to one side near the door, leaving my chair

empty.

Sheriff Albright said, "I'll let you gentlemen discuss the situation in private, for Chief Deputy Wright will a fill me in later." Albright shook hands with Calvins. "Glad you could join us . . . and welcome."

I did want to hang around long enough to catch at least some preliminaries of what Calvins might say.

Odell motioned to my now empty chair and Calvins sat down. He folded his hands on the table in front of him, and trained his eyes on Odell and then Balls. "The sheriff filled me in earlier on what's going down, and he mentioned that there was suspicion on your part that human trafficking might be involved." Calvins straightened his shoulders, sat a bit more erect.

Again, he peered from Balls to Odell and back again. "You're right on target on this. We've been building a case against a massive trafficking ring. They've got tentacles in at least five different states, and now it looks like they've moved into your area."

He twisted his head toward me, obviously debating as to how much more to say at the moment with me standing there.

Odell apparently sensed this and said to me, "Deputy Dorsey is right downstairs, and will run you back anytime you want."

"Yes, okay," I said. "Appreciate it." I knew this was my signal to leave. Balls' slightest nod of his head confirmed it. He'd fill me in later, I knew. "Glad to meet you, Agent Calvins," I said.

I left and closed the door behind me. Taking the back stairs, I met Deputy Dorsey in the hall.

"Ready to go?" he said.

"Sure thing."

His cell phone chirped, and he answered. I thought I might have time to slip down the hall and speak to Elly at work, but Dorsey's conversation lasted only a few seconds.

"That was Odell," he said. "Told me to stick with you."

We headed out the side door to his cruiser. Dorsey is in his twenties. A little chunky with an almost buzz cut of his reddish blond hair. His face is florid; a boyish glow to his skin. I've been around him before. I like him.

As I got in the passenger side of the cruiser, Dorsey said with a grin, "We're gonna go make some music." He started the car. "Lot better'n serving papers."

We chatted on the way up to my house. I learned that Dorsey was originally from the northern part of Currituck County in Moyock, and that he'd rarely left the area. He attended two years at the College of Albemarle before joining the sheriff's department.

When we got to my house, he waited down in the cruiser while I went upstairs. Told him I'd just be a few minutes and why didn't he come on up. He said he was fine just waiting. I had to make sure Janey had plenty of seeds, a fresh spring of millet and water. I went to the bathroom and washed my face, did a brief inspection of my hair and sort of brushed it. Good enough for jazz, I thought with a smile.

In my bedroom, I picked up my towel-wrapped revolver. I could carry it along with the bass. Balls was wise in saying for me to keep it with me.

Picking up the bass by the handle on the cover and securing the neck of the bass up against my shoulder, I made my way carefully down the outside steps, and went around to the rear of my Subaru Outback. Dorsey got out of the cruiser and offered to help. I told him I could manage. The backseats were already folded forward. With one hand I opened the trunk and slid the bass in on its back.

"We're ready," I said, flexing my shoulders.

Dorsey had watched the process. "That's a big instrument," he said.

"Yes, and it gets heavier every year," I said.

He looked puzzled at first, then began to grin.

He didn't question the dishtowel in my right hand. As I

got in the car, I slipped the revolver under my seat.

Dorsey followed me up Duck Road. For his sake, I kept strictly to the speed limit. At Scarborough Faire, we turned into the road on the far side and I found a parking space right behind Island Bookstore. Dorsey got one just beyond to the left. I went through the process of getting the bass out of the rear of the Outback, and walked the short distance on the wide wooden sidewalk to the front deck, where we would play. Dane was already there setting up his drums.

Carefully, I laid my bass down on its side and spoke to Dane. He was very slim and seemed to be all sharp elbows and shoulder blades. When he played, he bobbed his head in time to the music. His neck was skinny and looked barely able to support his tousled head and large eyes. He was a good, tasteful drummer, and augmented the music; not drowning it out.

Dorsey came up and I introduced him to Dane. "I'll sit down front," Dorsey said. "Play pretty."

By the time I'd unzipped the cover for my bass, Paul Settlemyer had arrived with his electronic keyboard. It was more of a real piano than many of the smaller keyboards that a lot of bands used.

Right behind him came Jim Watson, carrying his trumpet case and two music stands, one for him, one for me. Paul had his music with him. Jim supplied us with binders that contained fifty or more songs. He had put these binders together using pages from various so-called fake books.

Musicians used the fake books a lot. Basically, the pages consisted of simply the melody lines of a tune plus the chord symbols. I could use them quite well. If I hadn't memorized the tune and its chord structure, I could follow along and get by mostly by playing the root and fifth of a chord, maybe with a few notes of fill-in to spice it up.

Today there would be just the four of us. From time to time, we added Gordon McClaren on tenor sax or Steve Thomas on trombone. They contributed a great deal. But, heck, we did fine with the four of us.

Just before one, I tuned one string at a time while Paul prompted me with notes from the keyboard. I also checked my electronic tuner. The keyboard and my tuner were in sync with each other. Wanted to make sure. Jim adjusted the tuning slide on his horn. He was a tad sharp to start with. He made a tiny adjustment on his slide, hit an A-note, then a G. He nodded and said, "Close enough for jazz," a common expression among those with small combos.

We opened with our usual: a good solid rendition of "A Foggy Day." Nice medium upbeat. Next, we did Duke Ellington's "Satin Doll," a tune I really liked. We were drawing a crowd out front. Some stood around. Others sat at the tables and few chairs. We got nice applause.

A jazzy version of "Exactly Like You," then another fast tempo on "Lady Be Good."

We slowed things down with one of Jim's favorites, "Confessing." He did a nice bit with his horn and then launched into a somewhat guttural vocal: "I'm confessin' that I love you . . ."

It was then that I spotted my friend Betsy Robinson standing near the back and smiling big and applauding loudly. She's a great vocalist and I called Jim's attention to her when we finished his tune.

Jim motioned enthusiastically to Betsy. He took the microphone and urged the audience, which had grown a bit larger, to encourage Betsy to come sit in and give us a song or two. The audience responded with a hearty round of applause.

Betsy surrendered with a big grin and her upturned palms, and made her way toward the deck and the band.

When she was up on the deck, and thanked Jim and the audience. He asked her what she'd like to sing. She grinned back at me and said, "Let's do 'Fever.' A-minor."

I nodded and smiled. "The Peggy Lee version. Right?"

"Sure," she said.

Jim said to me, "Come on up front."

He knew, same as I did, that the tune featured only bass and drums—and the vocalist.

I brought my bass up near Betsy. She gave me a hug, made a little awkward because the bass was in the way.

"Ready to do it?" she said.

"Ready." Some years earlier I had listened to the Peggy Lee recording of "Fever" over and over until I had memorized the bass part and could play it fine. Loved the bass part, which, along with Peggy Lee's vocal, really made the tune. I nodded, and played the first few bars by myself, and then with rousing power, Betsy came in with the vocal . . . "Fever . . . You give me fever . . ."

Jim snapped his fingers in time, and Dane, as always, played tastefully, with an occasional sharp tap-tap of the snare.

When we finished, the crowd obviously loved it. I did too. Jim gave credit to me and to Dane and then asked Betsy if she'd do one more song. She agreed to do "Summertime."

"Also in A-minor," she said.

Jim played along on trumpet, giving terrific background riffs from time to time.

We were having fun.

After finishing, Jim and the audience thanked Betsy. She waved goodbye and threw me a kiss.

We took a very short break. I noticed that Deputy Dorsey had taken a cell phone call. He looked up at me, and then taking the side steps, he made his way around to where we were. Leaning in close to me, he said that he had to make a call back in Kill Devil Hills. He said Odell apologized for taking him away and for me to call the department when I got back home.

I said I would, and Dorsey hurried back toward the parking area.

And we kicked off some more tunes. The time went fast and at close to three, Jim called up the last two tunes. As always, we ended with "A Foggy Day," the tune we started with and our more or less theme song.

It didn't take long to break down and pack up. After I put my bass in the car, I went into the bookstore to browse around. I loved the way bookstores smell, and I breathed deeply when I went in. The staff was always friendly and greeted me warmly.

For once, I managed not to buy a book, said goodbye to the young woman behind the chest-high counter, and went to my Subaru. I kept a sharp lookout as I approached my car, got in and started the engine.

Before I backed out, I called Sam at the airport. Surprisingly I got her right away. She had just come back in from flying. "Sam, I've got to attend a press conference in the morning. I know this is short notice, but I wonder if maybe we can do a lesson on Friday rather than tomorrow."

She said to hold on a minute. When she came back on she said, "Can you do eight a.m.?"

"Absolutely," I said. "See you then."

I promised myself I was going to spread out my commitments a bit more. As often, it seemed I was trying to do too many different things and they begin to bump into each other if you crowd in too much.

Carefully, I backed out of the parking space behind Island Bookstore and began the circular drive out to the road. Large SUVs and a couple of pickup trucks parked at angles on both sides of the narrow lane made getting out of the parking area a bit of a challenge. Had to navigate slowly. Made it, then my left turn onto the side road and short distance farther and I stopped at Duck Road and tried to wait patiently for a break in the slow moving traffic to make another left and head south.

I was conscious of another vehicle that had come up behind me but most of my concentration was on the Duck Road traffic. There was a break in the approaching traffic on my left and that allowed me to move quickly into the center turn lane. The vehicle behind me made the same move and came up close behind me. It was a pickup truck. I wasn't sure whether it had been one of those in the Scarborough Faire parking area or not.

A kindly driver in the southbound lane paused and motioned for us to move ahead, which we did, almost in tandem. I waved a thank-you, even if the thoughtful driver couldn't see my hand. There's a lot of give and take in Duck on that road. Has to be. It's crowded and slow moving, especially in the summer.

At a marked pedestrian crossing fifty or seventy-five yards ahead, I had to stop as a family and then a lone elderly man made their way across Duck Road. The pickup truck was up close behind me. I tried to see the driver, but the way the light reflected on his windshield, it was impossible. I could only tell that it was a man and he was the only occupant.

As we got out of the main part of Duck, the traffic speeded up a bit. The pickup was close behind me. I don't like someone driving that close to me. I kept glancing in the rearview mirror.

And I tried not to let my imagination run away with me.

I decided that instead of continuing on Duck Road as I normally would, I would make a sudden turn off onto Hillcrest and take a back way through Southern Shores and past the Duck Woods Country Club to the Bypass.

We caught the stoplight just before Hillcrest. It turned green and a short distance farther I could see that the light at Hillcrest was green, too.

I slowed only slightly and—contrary to my ingrained usual practice—I didn't put my turn signal on but whipped right onto Hillcrest.

The pickup truck made the turn right behind me, and almost as fast.

Chapter Twenty

At the first four-way stop sign on Hillcrest, I pretended to be leaning forward to look both ways. I reached down under my seat and brought up the revolver and tucked it in my lap.

I drove forward, the truck right behind me. I still couldn't see the driver clearly. Another four-way stop sign at Hickory. I stopped, checked for traffic and then, again without engaging my turn signal, I accelerated rapidly onto Hickory. Then slowed immediately. Time for a showdown maybe? I took quick short breaths.

Then I breathed more normally because partially hidden in shrubbery off to the right, there was the welcome sight of a Southern Shores police cruiser. I checked my rearview mirror. The pickup driver paused a long moment at the stop sign. Apparently he had seen the police cruiser also.

The pickup truck then proceeded slowly through the intersection—and straight ahead.

I sighed with relief. But not complete relief. I knew the pickup could loop around and catch up with me when Hickory dead-ended at Dogwood Trail.

I lifted a hand in greeting at the cruiser as I drove slowly past. I hopped the cruiser would decide to follow me, but he didn't.

When I got up to the end of Hickory and stopped, there was no pickup truck in sight. I breathed almost normally, and slipped the revolver back under the seat. Maybe the driver of the pickup lived around here—and was an aggressive tailgater. Driving as badly as I was.

Okay. Paranoid, perhaps, but I had a damn good reason to be paranoid.

When I got home, I was completely over the anxiety caused by the tailgating pickup. I took my revolver under one arm and went around to the rear of the car to retrieve my bass. Carrying it up the backstairs is always a problem, much more so than going down the stairs. If I go up facing forward, I have to bend back at an uncomfortable and awkward angle to make sure the bottom of the instrument clears the steps. I could go up backward and clear the steps easily but that is even more awkward.

Without mishap, I got the bass in the house and didn't drop the revolver in the process. I laid the bass down on its side in the living room and took the gun back to the bedside table.

"Yes, Janey, I know you're glad to see me, and I'm glad to be home." She did her head-bobbing dance and chattered away.

I went to the phone. Time to call Elly and also check with Balls or Odell about tomorrow's press conference. Elly doesn't mind for me to call her at work; if she's busy she lets me know.

Elly's coworker Janet answered. I spoke to her and asked if Elly was busy. "Never too busy to talk to you," she said, and then in a singsong voice I heard her say, "Elly, there's someone special on the phone."

Elly said something to Janet and I heard Janet laugh and then Elly came on. She said, "I hope the playing went well."

"It did," I said.

Then Elly's voice dropped more softly. "You had no problems, did you?"

"Well, no," I said. "Wasn't expecting any."

"You sure? I mean not expecting any trouble?"

Uh-oh. She'd been talking with Mabel.

"I'm glad Deputy Dorsey was there with you," she said.

Yep, the word gets around fast.

"I guess you heard about a phone call I got?"

"Harrison, I can't help but worry about you. You know that. I mean, you are always getting yourself in danger."

"Well, no. Not always. And besides, Elly, with the press conference tomorrow, whoever made that call—and maybe it was just a prank—will know that I'm not the one looking into this . . . this investigation, so you know . . ." My voice trailed off. Of course I knew it wasn't a prank call, but I did believe that with the word getting out from the press conference, that I would not be considered the focus of the investigation. And I didn't think anyone would be dumb enough to start threatening Balls or Odell or any other of the lawmen.

"You know as well as I do that the call you received was not a hoax. Mabel said the sheriff didn't like it either. He took it seriously . . . and so should you!"

Her voice had risen a bit in volume.

"I do take it seriously, Elly," I said. "But by tomorrow, I really do think the word will be out and I won't be a . . . be a target for any sort of nut."

"Keep your doors locked and outside lights on tonight, please."

"I will," I said. "And, please, please try not to worry." I took a deep breath. "I'll call tonight after you've got Martin in bed. Tell you goodnight. Oh, and I'll see you in the morning at the courthouse. Hope you can make it to the press conference."

She sounded somewhat more placated. Not quite as worried, and really upset with me. I truly wondered about that from time to time; I mean the fact that what I do causes her anxiety and real worry. Am I being fair to her? I like being with her, and I love her, and I know she feels the same way, so maybe it's worth the occasional torment of worry and anxiety on her part. I hope so.

It was time to check in with Balls. I called his cell. He answered as always with, "Yeah?"

"You still in town?"

"Headed back home. Got a wife, you know." I heard road noise and the engine of his Thunderbird. His voice was a bit distorted because I could tell he was talking hands-free. "Be back in the morning for the press conference." Then another short pause and he said, "How did the cello playing go today? Anybody threaten you?"

"Playing the *bass fiddle* went well. No threats." Then I asked what I really wanted to know. "How did it go with Agent Calvins?"

Balls got more serious. "Very well. He's a good man and they've been doing more work than you'd think, and here in this area. He was tightlipped about the work, but he said he'd check with a higher up and felt like he'd be able to fill us in more tomorrow before the press conference."

"I'll be there," I said. "Before the press conference."

"Okay. I told him about the phone calls you've had and how you're sort of involved. He's okay with you being there in the morning for his briefing . . . long as you don't screw things up by running your mouth."

"I'll try not to," I said. "Curb my natural inclination for disrupting proceedings."

"You're a smartass," Balls said. But then he added, "Keep the doors locked tonight and keep that peashooter of yours handy."

Then I told Balls what I'd mentioned to Elly, that by tomorrow, with the press conference and all, whoever had called me would realize that I'm not the one doing the snooping, thus removing me as a target.

Balls said, "I agree." Another pause. "Gonna hang up. Just the same, tonight keep alert."

"Always," I said.

"Yeah, right."

I got up, stepped out on the deck and watched the sky fading. The sun now touching the tops of the pine trees to the west and south.

Going back inside, I locked and secured the sliding glass door, pulled the drapes closed, and went to the kitchen door and locked it.

"Okay, Janey, staying in tonight."

As plain as anything, she said, "Shit." And then did some more head bobbing.

"My sentiments exactly," I said.

After a light supper—and I mean really light; cold cereal and milk, with a sliced banana and cheese toast—I surfed TV for a bit of news or entertainment. I was in no mood to dig back into the writing. Maybe I'd try to get a few paragraphs in the morning before heading to Manteo and the courthouse.

At one point in the evening, I heard someone drive into the cul-de-sac, back up and leave.

Probably nothing. Someone had taken my road by mistake in all likelihood. I went quickly to the sliding glass door to peer outside. But the vehicle was not in sight. Could it have been the pickup again? Jeeze, but I was getting jumpy.

Chapter Twenty-One

I was up early Wednesday morning, showered and shaved and fixing a bagel, orange juice and sausage patty. Janey chirped away as I scurried about in the kitchen. She loved the commotion.

By eight o'clock I prepared to head down to the car. I got on the first steps and then remembered my revolver and went back in the bedroom, retrieved it, and took it with me. Tell the truth, I felt a tad foolish lugging that handgun around with me. But, oh well.

I started to get in the car when I noticed a cigarette butt in my driveway a couple of feet from the rear of the car. I stepped back to look at it. I have two neighbors in the cul-de-sac but I didn't think they smoked. Maybe they did, or maybe they had guests who did. At any rate, someone was standing there smoking during the night.

In the console of my Subaru, I had a small package of tissues. I took one and picked up the cigarette butt. Why, I wasn't sure. DNA or something? Get real, Harrison. Just the same, I saved it, wrapped in the tissue, and put it in the console.

I drove slightly above the speed limit toward Manteo. I wanted to be there no later than eight-thirty. Nose my way into a meeting with Balls, Odell, and FBI Agent Calvins.

Parking on Sir Walter Raleigh Street close to the courthouse, I hurried to the front porch. Inside the hall, Elly was opening her office door. She glanced over her shoulder. No one was around. So we went into a quick embrace and a light kiss on the lips. She grinned.

"Nice way to start the workday," she said.

"Lovely way," I said. "You smell good." She always did. Reminded me always of fresh cotton and sunshine.

"Maybe tonight," she said as she stepped into her office.

"Let's count on it."

I hurried upstairs. As I expected, Balls was already there. He and Odell sat in the interrogation room with the door open. They had brought in an extra chair, so there was room for four of us. That was a good sign.

I nodded, shook hands with Odell and tapped Balls on the shoulder.

"You oversleep?" he said.

"And good morning to you, Balls," I said.

"Okay," he said to me as I took one of the chairs, "Agent Calvins has agreed to have you in here for this briefing since you've managed to get yourself involved right from the beginning, but that doesn't mean you can run your mouth. Sit there and act polite."

"I'll do my best."

He made that "humpf" sound.

We heard Sheriff Albright talking with someone in the hall. Agent Calvins, I assumed.

Mabel stuck her head in the door. "Now don't think I do this often, but I've got four coffees coming."

"Thank you, Mabel," Odell said.

In a few minutes, a young woman who helped Mabel from time to time, brought in a tray with four coffees, cream and sugar.

The sheriff and Calvins were still outside chatting. I heard the sheriff say, "I'll be in there shortly. Give you a chance to talk with them, fill them in, and I'll come in before we're ready for the press conference. Set the ground rules."

"Yes, sir, Sheriff," Agent Calvins said.

I had pulled my chair a few feet to the right of Balls so I didn't look like I was part of the official gathering, but more of a permitted visitor. Which I was.

Calvins came in. Our FBI agent. And he still looked the part. This was despite that he had shed his dress shirt and tie and wore a green and yellow sport shirt that appeared brand new. His slacks were surely part of a suit. Complete with cuffs. He was trying to blend in, but he didn't quite make it. Not sure what it was. Maybe his neatly trimmed and combed hair. I don't know. He didn't look scruffy enough for the Outer Banks. Outsider was written all over him. Federal Agent, too.

He had a warm smile and he shook hands with each of us and told Balls he was glad to see him again.

He sat in the extra chair and crossed one leg over the other. Once again, he smiled and nodded to Odell and to me. "I'm glad that we can have a little chat before the press conference," he said, "so that we can establish something of a scenario."

Balls said, "We are too, and before the press conference, we'd really like your perspective on what's going on."

"I understand, and I think that's certainly in order," Calvins said. "You should know, and probably do, that I've been working on this investigation with two agents from Homeland Security. Good investigators, too."

Odell said, "We'd certainly appreciate you telling us what you think."

Calvins leaned forward, his arms on the table, hands splayed out in front of him. He studied his hands a moment, then glanced at each of us in turn. "It's no secret what I think, or what the agents from Homeland Security think. I talked with Sheriff Albright about it, and it's the same thing that you, Odell and Agent Twiddy, have discussed. And that's human trafficking. A whole network. A really sophisticated operation. And we think a kingpin of the operation is here at the Outer Banks."

So now it was out and getting official.

Calvins continued, "And that homicide of Findley—the one who called Mr. Weaver—was obviously connected to the human trafficking, and we have every reason to believe that those two missing young women were trafficked . . . and sold into prostitution."

Balls cleared his throat, signaling that he wanted to say something. Calvins paused and turned to Balls. Balls said, "This latest death—the woman found along the roadside—appears to be a homicide, also. At least there's strong evidence of it."

Calvins cocked his head, waiting for Balls to continue.

"The autopsy performed over in Greenville shows that she died from a lethal overdose of drugs, heroin and some other fancy stuff."

Calvins wrinkled his brow. "Maybe self-inflicted?"

Balls said, "Maybe. But there was no prior indication she was a user. Dr. Mordecai found two needle marks in her back. The coroner here had already seen one. One in her lower back and one center of the upper back. She couldn't stick a needle back there. Someone else did." He shook his head, a half-smile hardly there. "And she didn't dump herself alongside the road."

Despite Balls admonition for me to keep quiet, I couldn't any longer since there was already a lot of speculation going around. "That young woman who drowned—Marisa—was supposed to be going to a party just like those other two were, and maybe the same party. I think she realized what was happening—that they were being sold—and she either jumped overboard to escape . . . or they threw her overboard."

All three of them looked at me. I couldn't tell what they were thinking. Then Calvins spoke up: "That's not as far-fetched as it might sound. If that's true, then all three deaths and the missing two women are all part of the same thing."

I could tell that Balls mentally chewed on something. "Okay, Larry," he said, "tell us more about how you and those guys from Homeland Security have come up with all of this. Not that we haven't thought the same thing. But it sounds like you might even have a line on who is behind it all." He attempted what could pass as a friendly, encouraging smile.

Agent Calvins grinned it him and appeared stalling for time to weigh exactly how much he was going to say. "Well, to be perfectly honest with you, Ballsford, there's a limit on how much I can say until I coordinate with the Homeland investigators. I can say, however, that we believe one of the ringleaders is right here in this area."

Calvins went on. "Using the tried and true method of investigation, we've followed the money. And those Homeland Security guys have more leeway than we in the Bureau have with the ability to 'follow the money.' They can zero in on it—domestic and offshore accounts. Some of that money—and we're talking really big bucks—is traced back to the Outer Banks."

"Yeah? Don't suppose you can give us a name?" Balls said. His question was not challenging—exactly. But there was a tone of aggression that I recognized.

"Afraid not at this juncture. Maybe we'll have one soon. Hope so." He turned a smile at Balls, apparently trying to indicate he wanted to cooperate.

Odell said, "Agent Calvins you mentioned they were selling the women into prostitution. Where?"

I wasn't sure that Calvins was going to respond; he delayed so long, again studying his outstretched hands.

"We're fairly certain that some of the women are sold offshore. Taken out to sea where they meet another boat and are transferred—provided a lot of cold cash is exchanged. And I'm talking about tens of thousands of dollars, especially for blondes from Eastern Europe and Russia."

"Jesus," Odell whispered.

Balls nodded. I don't believe this intelligence was totally new to his thinking, that he suspected as much.

Slave trade, I thought. Pure and simple slave trade. And evil as hell.

Calvins said, "The girls are drugged, either willingly or forced. They get hooked and never get away."

The door opened and Sheriff Albright stood there. "Getting close to when we need to gather for the press conference. But let's talk about how much we're going to say."

"Yes, sir," Odell said.

"Have a seat, Sheriff," I said, vacating my chair and standing away from the table.

"No, thanks. I'm fine standing." He straightened his shoulders, sucked in his stomach. He looked good in his khaki uniform; not his full-dress uniform, but a neat and well-creased one. "We've got at least four or five reporters coming and they want to know about the latest death and whether it's a homicide and also about Thomas Findley . . . and I've got a feeling that someone's going to ask if they are connected, and maybe even about human trafficking since those two women are missing." He sighed audibly. "We've got to be prepared for those questions and decide how much we're going to say."

Odell turned to Balls and then to Calvins. No one spoke for a few seconds, and then Calvins said, "Well, I plan to be among those in the audience. I don't need to be up there with you, Sheriff . . . or with Deputy Odell or with Agent Twiddy."

"All right," Albright said. "I'll have an opening statement. Odell and Agent Twiddy can be up there with me so I can turn to them if I need to." He chuckled. "And I'm pretty sure I'll need to."

Balls spoke up. "I would suggest, Sheriff, it's always safe to say that this is an ongoing investigation and we're considering every possibility." Balls inclined his head toward Agent Calvins. "And if anyone wants to know about calling in the FBI you can always say we can use all the help possible."

Calvins said, "I hope no one mentions the Bureau. I would much rather stay completely anonymous."

"But if we're asked outright?" Sheriff Albright said. "I'm not going to deny it."

"Let's play it as it falls," Balls said. "It's not a hostile bunch of reporters . . . generally."

The sheriff nodded, took a deep breath, and said, "Okay. It's show time. Let's head on to the courtroom."

Chapter Twenty-Two

Mabel was already setting up for the press conference when we went in. She had the wooden podium up front with eight chairs lined up facing the podium. These were for reporters. She had signs on the backs of a couple of chairs that said "Media." There were plenty of chairs in the back for spectators, if there were any, and I expected that there would be a dozen or more.

Shortly before ten o'clock, Linda Shackleford arrived, now representing *The Outer Banks Sentinel*. It was satisfying to see how in three or four short years she had progressed from photos and classified ads, to a reporter and photographer with *The Coastland Times* and now had recently joined *The Sentinel* as an investigative reporter and feature writer.

We shared a quick hug. She's a long-time friend of Elly's. That's how I first met Linda. She's sturdy and has strong large teeth that I've always thought looked like they could chew through rawhide.

Other reporters, chatting with each other as they entered, took seats up front along with Linda. I drifted toward the back and took a seat next to Agent Larry Calvins, who sat at the far end of one of the rows.

Other reporters included the new young man with *The Coastland Times*, Jeff Hubbard of *The Virginian-Pilot*, Shirley Smothers from *The Daily Advance* of Elizabeth City,

Mary Ann Little of the weekly *Camford Courier* from Currituck County, and a radio reporter I didn't know. He had attached a portable recorder to the podium.

Several courthouse regulars from the town took seats in the back, along with a young lawyer I knew. I kept an eye out for Elly, thinking she might very well slip up here for part of the press conference.

At ten, Sheriff Albright spoke privately to Odell and Balls as the three of them stood together near the podium but behind it. Then Albright approached the podium. Odell and Balls stood erect behind him and to his right. Albright held a single sheet of paper in his hand. With his free hand he made a passing brush at the cowlick at the crown of his head. It didn't do much good.

All conversation in the room had stopped. Albright cleared his throat and welcomed everyone for coming. "I have a brief statement and then we'll take a few questions," he said.

Albright adjusted his glasses and made a quick visual pass at the piece of paper on the podium. "As you know, we had a homicide last week of one Thomas Findley, who was killed with shots to the head and body. And this week we discovered the body of one Micki Mitchell over on the mainland near Mann's Harbor alongside Highway 64. While we don't have all of the details of the cause of her death, pending a complete autopsy, there is evidence of foul play. So in effect, we have two homicides—one a definite and one a possible homicide—under active investigation."

Jeff Hubbard raised his hand, but Albright indicated with a wave of his own hand that he was not quite through with his opening statement.

Albright continued. "At this time, we do not have suspects, but we will keep you informed with press statements as we progress. And I'm sure we will make progress. Chief Deputy Odell Wright is the lead on this investigation, expertly assisted by Agent Ballsford Twiddy of the State Bureau of Investigation." He cleared his throat again and peered over the top of his glasses. "This concludes my opening statement."

Jeff Hubbard's hand shot back up.

"Yes?"

"Sheriff, do you believe that these two deaths are connected? I mean you mention both of them in your statement. Are you thinking there's a connection?"

"We're looking into all possibilities," Albright said. "I can say that on the surface, there doesn't seem to be any connection." He tried something of a dismissive smile. "But since we're looking into both, I wanted to bring you up to date about what we're working on."

Linda Shackleford raised her hand.

"Yes, Linda?"

"Sheriff, I know you've had a report of two missing young women. Any progress on that investigation?"

Albright paused as if studying something on his podium. "No, Linda. No real progress. But let me have Chief Deputy Odell Wright address that question."

He turned to Odell, who tried to hide an expression of surprise; I could tell Odell attempted to formulate something of a response as he approached the podium beside Albright. "We're actively pursuing leads on the two missing women. At this juncture, we haven't settled on specific theories. As I say, it is an ongoing investigation."

He appeared to be ready to say something else when Jeff Hubbard spoke up without raising his hand. "Do you think they were, like, abducted? Or maybe decided they'd had enough of the beach? I mean, decided to leave the area?"

Odell waited a moment before he answered, obviously carefully crafting his response. "After checking with the women's roommates, and inspecting their living quarters, we are convinced—or virtually certain—the two women did not plan to vacate the beach area."

Hubbard spoke again: "How can you be 'virtually certain'?"

Odell appeared irritated by the follow-up question, but he hid it well. "As I said, we inspected their living quarters." With an indication he was ended the inquiry, he said, "It's an ongoing investigation."

Albright came to the rescue. "Perhaps you media folks can help us on this. You know, ask your readers to contact you if they have any information that might lead to where these two women might be. That sort of thing." Then, as if an afterthought, he said, "When we finish here, if you're interested, Odell can give you the full names of the women and something of a physical description."

Jeff Hubbard nodded his head as if this satisfied him.

Albright was obviously about to wind up the briefing, when Mary Ann Little tentatively fluttered a hand up. "Yes?" Albright said.

"Sheriff Albright, I know there has been a lot of talk lately about human trafficking. One of the papers in the area even had a series on it, and I was wondering, sir, if you have any reason to suspect that these two women are victims of human trafficking?"

Uh-oh. This is what we hoped might not come up.

Albright fumbled with the paper sheet in front of him. Then he plastered a smile on his face and said, "I think this is a question that SBI Agent Twiddy might address."

Balls stepped forward and Albright, with obvious relief, retreated from the podium. Balls said, "We're actively considering all possibilities as to what might have happened to the two women, where they might have gone . . . either voluntarily or involuntarily. But at this point there is no way we can definitively make any assessments."

Okay, Balls handled that well, without saying a damn thing.

I looked around the room. Elly had come in and stood near the rear door. She smiled.

Balls moved back from the podium and Albright took

over once again. "I think that about wraps it up, ladies and gentlemen. Thank you for coming . . ."

Linda Shackleford stood and held up a finger. "One last question, Sheriff. There's a rumor going around that you may be involving the FBI on this investigation—or these investigations, plural. Is this so?"

Albright swallowed. I'm sure he did his best not to automatically look back toward FBI Agent Calvins, who had tried to shrink his frame into the chair.

"Linda, I'm not going to go into every detail of what we are trying to do or what we may find it necessary and prudent to do. We've got an outstanding team of investigators right here. If it becomes necessary then, yes, we will involve other sources." He bobbed his head. "Okay, thank all of you for coming." He picked up his single sheet of paper and retreated.

No more questions.

And certainly, no more answers.

Chapter Twenty-Three

As the reporters gathered to leave, I spoke to Linda Shackleford and then made my way over to Mary Ann Little of the *Camford Courier*. I had only spoken to her maybe once before. She seemed almost shy, but she smiled and held out her hand. With the other hand she brushed back a lock of hair on the right side of her head that didn't appear to want to behave.

I reintroduced myself. "Please give my regards to your boss," I said. The editor and publisher of her paper was Thaddeus Sinclair, whom I had known back in DC when he was with *The Washington Post*. Following a lifelong dream, he bought a small weekly newspaper and the print shop that went with it and moved up the road from the Outer Banks at Camford Courthouse. He was an excellent journalist and a nice guy. Mary Ann was lucky to be working for him.

"I certainly will," she said and relaxed a bit.

Elly had disappeared. She'd returned to her office, I was sure.

I made my way back to the sheriff's office. Balls, Odell, and Calvins. had gathered there. The sheriff sat behind his desk, questioning the trio about how they thought the press conference went.

Calvins said, "Under the circumstances, I thought it went very well." He appeared relieved, "We're lucky they're not as aggressive as some reporters I've dealt with."

"It's a good bunch," Balls said. "And they do a good job without being real pains in the ass."

Sheriff Albright looked at me. "You haven't had any more of those threatening calls have you?"

"No, sir." I'll admit I thought about blurting out about the suspicious pickup truck, as well as the cigarette butts near my driveway. But, even in my mind, it sounded lame, and I decided to keep quiet.

Balls said, "Now that it's obvious that Weaver here is not a Lone Ranger on the investigations, my belief is that he's no longer a target."

"I agree," Calvins said, and Odell nodded his head.

"I'll leave you gentlemen," I said, "and get back home to get to work."

To me, Balls said, "Stop downstairs first and speak to someone." He grinned.

"Plan to," I said.

And I did. Elly finished talking with a young paralegal and put away one of the hefty record books.

She came to the counter. I leaned close. "An interesting press conference," she said. "I'm not sure what was said. I mean what news was given, but at least the reporters didn't get unruly."

I agreed. "From a reporter's standpoint, there wasn't much. From the sheriff's view, it's about what he wanted."

That smile of hers was still there. "I watched the FBI agent. I almost laughed. I've never seen anyone as big as he is try to become so invisible."

Elly's coworker, Janet, spoke to one of the young attorneys who came in.

"I'd better let you get to work," I said. "Tonight? Can I pick you up about six? You and I'll go out to eat. A real grownup date?"

"Sounds good," she said. There was almost a wink as I left and she went back to work.

I drove home and actually got a lot of work done on the piece I was writing. Didn't wind up the work until time to take a shower and get dressed. The weather was August warm and I called Elly and said, "Casual."

"Yes," she said. "I'm going to wear shorts if that's okay."

"Same here," I said.

By five-thirty I was in my car and headed south on the Bypass to Manteo. Arrived at Elly's house right at six. I got out and went up on the little porch. I was about to tap on the screen door when Elly opened the door with Martin standing beside her, hanging onto one of her bare legs. She looked great in the tailored stone-colored shorts and pink pullover cotton collared top. Her hair was pulled back loosely, exposing her neck, which I loved to see.

Martin eyed me suspiciously. He knew I was getting ready to whisk his mother away.

Mrs. Pedersen came to the door and told Martin that the two of them were going to have ice cream. He appeared to think about it a moment. Elly patted his head; he shrugged and apparently decided on the ice cream rather than hanging on to his mother's leg and doing a weepy protest as she left with this . . . this man, whom he tolerated from time to time.

With a cheery goodbye to Martin and a thank-you to Mrs. Pedersen, Elly accompanied me to my car. I opened the door for her.

"Thank you, kind sir," she said.

We drove away. I said, "The Rundown Café? We haven't been there in a while."

"Fine," she said.

On the drive up to Kitty Hawk and The Rundown Café, we chatted about many things but rather surprisingly we barely touched on the investigation that Elly knew had been occupying my mind and my time.

But as we pulled into the parking lot at the café, Elly sat there a moment and turned her head toward me, fixing her eyes on mine. "Okay, Harrison, what do you think happens next? More young women go missing? Another killing or two? And what about the FBI agent? Has he really got leads?"

With a lopsided grin, I shook my head. "Golly, Elly, that's a lot of questions all at once." Then I got more serious. "Actually, it *is* sort of a wait and see thing for right now. I do believe Agent Calvins has someone—a person or persons of interest—that he's not telling about. At least he hasn't given any identity in my presence. Maybe he has homed in on a suspect. And I surely hope there'll be no more killings . . . or women disappearing." A sad shake of my head. "But until this thing is wrapped up, I'm afraid there might be more . . . more activity."

Now she was one the one to shake of her head. "You call it 'activity.' That's trying to put a pretty face to it, Harrison."

"Yes, I know."

She put her hand on the door handle, then smiled, along with another shake of her head. "Let's go get something to eat."

We went in and got seated upstairs at the bar area where we had a view of the ocean. Elly ordered the soft chicken tacos and I got coconut shrimp. It was good and we ate and listened to the lively activity around us.

Toward the end of our meal I spoke up to say what I'd been thinking of for some time. "Maybe we can swing by my house before you have to scurry home?"

Elly put her fork down and tilted her head toward me. With an expression of mock disapproval, she said, "I think you might have something wicked in mind."

Couldn't help but grin. "Yes, I do," I said.

She returned my grin. "Well, I'm about finished eating. We going to hang around here all night?"

I signaled our server. "Check?" I mouthed.

We drove down the Beach Road to Kitty Hawk Road

and went up to the Bypass and the couple of more miles to my house. We talked very little. At one point Elly reached over and put her left hand gently on my forearm. I guess we're both sort of old fashioned. We are very circumspect and, yes, discreet, about stealing away some time to be intimately with each other. And it's not frequent enough to be blasé about it when we can be together. A bit of nervous tension, maybe. Anticipation. I attribute it to, as I said, being somewhat old fashioned, but also there's Martin, and Elly remains the devoted and caring mother. And on top of that, this is a small community in many ways, and Elly is well known. I guess I am also, to a certain extent.

Ain't like in the movies where the couple rolls around in bed before the first reel has run its course.

Holding hands, we started up the outside steps to my house. Then we had to release hands because the stairway doesn't lend itself to walking side-by-side.

When we went inside, Elly said, "I'm going to get a glass of water." There was a jug of cold water in the refrigerator and I poured some for her and for myself. She drank half a glass quickly.

Janey chirped and eyed the two of us.

"She doesn't like me," Elly said.

"Jealous," I said. "She knows I'm crazy about you."

"Well, she can just live with it," Elly said, and she embraced me and we kissed hungrily.

"Oh, my," she said as we parted.

I took her hand and we went into the bedroom.

We both began shedding our clothes. Summertime, that didn't take long.

I took both of her hands in mine and we stood there and I admired her and looked her all over. "God, but you're lovely," I whispered. "I could devour you."

She got a mischievously wicked smile and said, "Be my guest."

I wrapped my arms about her and held her close and she

said "Oh, my" again and we stumbled toward the bed.

Later as we lay there, she raised herself on one elbow to check the clock on my bedside table.

"I know," I said.

"One of these days maybe we won't have to worry so much about the time." She said it with a touch of wistfulness in her voice.

"We didn't have to worry about it when we were in Paris."

"Yes, but that seems like a long time ago."

I knew, and she did too, that one of these days we were going to have to make a real decision. These almost stolen moments were wonderful. But we couldn't go on forever this way. I'm sure we both realized we would have to be together more permanently at some point—or these times together . . . oh, I don't know what. Would they become too superficial? I really didn't know. And maybe she didn't either.

Elly eased out of bed and gathered her clothes and said, "I'll be right back." She went in the bathroom and closed the door.

I got dressed.

Golly, was I somewhat depressed? I should be really happy. Maybe I was thinking too much.

She came back in the room and smiled. Perhaps I imagined it, but there seemed to be the edge of sadness in her smile.

"Yes, I know," I said again. "We've got to go."

Janey was quiet when we walked by her cage. She kept her eyes on Elly. "Goodnight, Janey," Elly said. "I'm leaving now so you can be happy again."

Janey made a low clucking sound and then was perfectly quiet.

We started toward the door and Elly stopped and looked around at the kitchen, the table I used for my office, the living room, the bass lying on its side. With a brief nod of her chin, she said, "You know, Harrison, one of these days . . ." She let her voice trail.

One more time that night I said, "Yes, I know."

Chapter Twenty-Four

Friday morning I was up early, showered, dressed in older shorts than I'd worn the night before, equally old golf shirt, and maybe even in older sneakers, and headed for the airport for my flying lesson with Samantha Inez Davis.

I got to the Manteo airport about eight forty-five. Sam leaned against the counter talking to the man on duty. She turned when I came in. "Ready to go flying?" she said with a smile.

"Looks like a good day for it. Sunny, very light wind,"

"Come on," she said and led the way out of the lounge to the porch and over toward the Cessna 172 parked on the right, nose pointing toward the building. "I've already done a preflight check, but that doesn't make any difference. You go through the whole thing—as always."

"Got it," I said.

Before we reached the aircraft, Sam stopped in mid-stride, turned to me. "Any progress yet on Micki's death?" She referred, of course, to the woman who had worked for her boyfriend.

I shook my head. "Not that I've heard since yesterday. It's being treated as a homicide."

"That's what Robert said. He talked with a Deputy Wright. He knows him. Robert said there were needle marks." Sam took a breath and we continued on toward the

Cessna. Over her shoulder, Sam said, "Robert said Micki might have smoked some pot but didn't do heavy drugs."

I nodded. There was nothing I needed to say or to add.

"Okay," Sam said as we stood alongside the aircraft, "start your preflight check."

I could smell the early morning sun on the fuselage and wings and the faint odor of aviation fuel. It was all a pleasant aroma. It felt comfortable and excitingly familiar I realized. The airplane smell. The machine that would take us aloft, dancing on the skies.

Starting on the pilot's side of the plane, I did the complete preflight check that Sam insisted on—fuel samples, stall horn, pitot tube, all connections, free movement of ailerons, stabilizer, oil, the works. Same sequence every time so it became totally ingrained.

We got in and buckled up. Put on the headsets so we could talk with each other . . . and others.

She nodded.

I opened my door and called out, "Clear prop," and I started the engine. This time I did a better job of taxiing out to take a position at the end of the south runway, our back to the Croatan Sound. We'd checked the wind earlier: light from the northeast, the direction in which we would be taking off. Using the toe brakes, I held the plane in place and ran the rpm up to about 2500, checking the functions; switched on carb heat and cycled the two magnetos. Everything good to go.

Since Manteo is an uncontrolled airport—no tower with air traffic controllers—Sam had me broadcast intentions of takeoff on CTAF, or common traffic advisory frequency, and scan around to make sure there was no traffic.

"Okay," she said, and I released the toe brakes and ran the power back up. I was pleased, too, that this time I kept the aircraft straight as we picked up speed down the runway. Not much wobbling. Sam makes me keep my right hand on the throttle to make sure it doesn't start to slip on takeoff, reducing power.

When I could feel we were at about takeoff speed and the plane wanted to get in the air, I gave a bit of backpressure on the yoke and we were airborne.

Always an exhilarating sensation. Pulse was up and a trace of a grin as we cleared the trees at the end of the runway, leaving them behind. Sam had me make a couple of shallow turns shortly after takeoff to scan for any approaching traffic.

We headed northwest toward the Wright Memorial Bridge and climbed to seven hundred-fifty feet. While many instructors would add at least another thousand feet to the training altitude, Sam was satisfied with our flying at that level in the beach area.

When we got to the Wright Memorial Bridge that connects Currituck and Dare counties, I made a turn toward the east and the ocean shoreline. I looked down at the waters of the Currituck Sound and the way sunlight sparkled at the top of the small swells. The water was relatively smooth, good for boating, and there was one waterman out working his crab pots.

When I made the turn, Sam said, "Keep your altitude."

I had drifted down a bit in the turn, and I eased the plane back up and kept an eye out to the side, back and forth, to make sure I kept my wingtips on the horizon so I was flying straight and level.

Sam said, "Go on down to Bodie Lighthouse. When you get there, I want you to circle the lighthouse, keeping your right wingtip pointed at the lighthouse. Keep circling, hold your attitude."

I nodded, and kept silent.

When shortly the lighthouse came into view, I edged toward it.

"Okay," she said. "Begin circling. Wingtip pointing at the top of the lighthouse."

I started the maneuver.

"You're going to have to bank sharply," she said.

I felt my shoulders and hands tensing up. I was doing a pretty sloppy job.

"When you head into the wind, the plane is going to want to rise. Compensate. Just the reverse will happen on downwind." She glanced at the altimeter and pointed a finger at it. "Altitude," she said.

We were banking at about thirty degrees. I did marginally better this time around. Still sloppy.

The third time around I did even better.

"Not too bad," she said.

I breathed a bit easier.

"Head toward Wanchese," she said. "Then the airport."

About five miles out, she told me to switch radio frequencies and announce over CTAF that we were coming in for a landing.

"Start easing it down," she said. Then she spoke over the CTAF and said we would do a touch-and-go.

I swallowed, and looked over at her.

"You can do it," she said.

I wasn't at all sure.

"Take it downwind toward the sound, do the base leg, and start lining up with the runway," she said.

I watched the altimeter. We were losing altitude, as she instructed. I made the turn over the sound and began the descent toward the runway. It looked like it came up very fast.

"Thirty degree flaps," she said.

I switched the toggle for the flaps and felt the plane slow.

"You're fine," she said.

I didn't feel like I was.

"Come on down."

The edge of the runway was below me.

"Ease it down," she said.

I noticed she kept her fingers on the yoke, just in case.

I tried to judge how far I was above the runway, which

seemed to be slipping past me at more speed that I thought.

"Less power," she said.

The plane wanted to keep on flying.

"Touch down," she said, and I pushed forward a tad on the yoke and we bounced hard on the runway—and up again. "Power up," she said, "and take off again. Go around." She flipped the toggle switch and raised the flaps.

We lifted off the runway, cleared the trees at the end and I banked and went back downwind toward the sound.

"Okay," Sam said. "You get some of the feeling. Do the base leg and I'll take over to bring us in. But I want you to keep your hands on the yoke—very lightly—so you can get a feel of how I'm doing it."

We landed smoothly.

I shook my head and grinned. "Like spreading peanut butter on a piece of bread," I said.

She grinned in return. "Takes practice. You'll get the hang of it—after about five hundred or so landings." Then she said, "Okay, taxi us back and park."

I didn't do too bad a job of getting off the runway and going back toward the main building and parking the plane in its usual spot and cutting the engine.

We got out and walking back toward the building I felt like I'd done a full day's work.

"Good lesson," she said. "You're coming along."

I walked a little straighter. Kind of proud.

Inside, she made notations in my logbook and put down the time we'd flown and described in a sort of shorthand, the exercises we'd done. Well, I was getting a few hours in.

We chatted a bit. The young man behind the counter grinned at me and said, "That was a nice little bounce you did on the touch-and-go."

"I was hoping not too many people saw that," I said. We laughed.

Sam checked her schedule. "Tuesday or Wednesday?" she said.

"Tuesday will probably be good. Let me call you later today or tomorrow morning to make sure."

"Fine," she said. Then more privately to me: "That investigation?"

I shrugged. "I'm not officially a part of it."

"I know, but . . ."

"Yes," I said.

After a while I left the airport and drove toward the courthouse. I turned up Budleigh Street and drove slowly by the west side of the courthouse. I didn't see Balls' car but there was a dark Dodge sedan parked in one of the reserved spots. I figured it probably belong to FBI Agent Calvins. I went around to the other side of the courthouse and found a space on Sir Walter Raleigh Street close to Downtown Books.

I went in the front of the courthouse and right to the Register of Deeds office. Elly talked to coworker Janet, and handed Janet a piece of paper. Then Elly saw me and smiled and came to the counter. Janet wiggled her fingers at me as a hello, and took the piece of paper back into the small adjoining office.

"How did the flying lesson go?" Elly said.

"Fine," I said. "Got a lot to learn, but Sam is patient . . . and a very good instructor."

"Attractive, too, isn't she?" Elly tilted her head in mock disapproval—or warning.

I grinned. "I hadn't noticed."

"Yeah, right." Then, "Seriously, was it a good lesson?"

"Yes, it was. She had me approach to land, and then takeoff again."

"Landing is supposed to be the hardest part, isn't it?"

"I can vouch for that," I said. I paused and leaned a little closer to the counter. "I know it's early for lunch, but want to go over to Poor Richard's for a sandwich?"

She said, "Remember? I've got to take Martin to the pediatrician's for his checkup. Make sure all is in order for preschool."

"Oh, yes. I'd forgotten. Preschool. I guess it is not too long before that time."

"I can hardly believe it," Elly said. "Time goes too fast . . . way too fast."

I wished good luck to Elly, said goodbye, and went across the street to Poor Richard's for a sandwich. Instead of just water, I splurged for sweet tea. Figured I could use the sugar after the flying lesson. And I did play over the lesson in my mind, thinking of the things I did right . . . and wrong. A lot to learn and I know, like a musical instrument, it takes practice, practice, practice.

Then I thought about the ongoing investigation. I tried not to think about that because, after all, it certainly wasn't my investigation and it wasn't as if it were in limbo. I mean, there's Balls, Odell and even the FBI involved in it. What business do I have pondering it? Well, I do have some business—my writing business, and I knew I would do a full piece on this when it finally winds up, and I do think it will wind up.

My sandwich came. Piled high with cheese and ham and lettuce and tomato—a nice slice of tomato—and mayonnaise. And a tall glass of sweet tea.

I dug in.

And speaking of writing, instead of sitting here replaying flying and thinking about *their* investigation, I needed to get myself in gear and finish up the piece I was working on for my editor Rose.

I had about finished my sandwich—the place was filling up with the lunch crowd—when my cell phone chirped. I checked the ID. It said "Clare's" and that puzzled me for a moment until I remembered I'd given hostess Terri my business card when I was there.

I answered but the connection was not good and there was a growing amount of chatter there in Poor Richard's.

"Let me call you right back," I said.

Signaling for the check, I paid, took a last bite of my sandwich and a swallow of sweet tea, and went outside. Off to the right there was a bench at a grassy area, and I sat there and called Terri.

"Hold a minute," she said.

I heard her talking to customers and, apparently, she seated them and came back to the phone. "Mr. Weaver? Sorry to keep you waiting."

"Yes, this is Weav. Mister isn't necessary, Terri. You know that."

"Yeah, yeah," she said. "I know you were interested in that woman, the mature woman who talked with the girls here."

She had my attention. "Yes?" I said.

"Well, I told you I hadn't seen her, but she came in today, early. She usually came at the end of lunch. But she was here. Didn't stay too long." She took a breath. "But long enough. I got her picture."

Now she really had my attention. "What? You did?"

That mischievous chuckle again. "Yeah, with my phone. I pretended to be taking a picture of one of the girls standing at the end of the counter, but I shifted a bit and got her." She exhaled a puff of breath. "A good one, too, if I do say so."

"Send it to me? Please."

"Coming to you. Email?"

"Fine." While she was getting ready to do that, I asked quickly, "What was the woman doing? Talking up other waitresses?"

"Yeah, she was." Then she added, "But we call them *servers*, not waitresses."

"Sorry," I said.

"Sending it now," she said, "and then I gotta go. Getting busy."

"Thanks so much, Terri. I really appreciate it."

"Bye, sweetie."

I waited, holding my phone, but trying not to look at it until I got the signal for incoming email.

A couple of breaths later I got the signal. Shading the screen on my phone with one hand so I could see the image better, I stared at the face of the woman.

I inhaled quickly, covered the screen with my hand and stared off toward the water a moment.

Then I looked again at the screen.

The woman was apparently speaking to one of the young women who stood there to take her order. Terri had zoomed in closer to the woman's face.

I recognized her. I knew exactly who she was. No question about it.

I thought about what that meant.

Yes, the matronly, almost grandmother woman sitting there, the one who had spent a number of lunches there at Clare's talking with the young women who disappeared, was Eunice Cleave, the sister of Basil Cleave who owned the big boat.

Eunice and Basil Cleave had to be involved. I was certain of it.

Chapter Twenty-Five

I didn't waste any more time sitting there. Making sure I saved the picture on my phone, I headed to the courthouse.

As I went by Elly's office, I saw that she had already left for the appointment with the pediatrician. I scurried up the stairs and poked my head into Mabel's office.

She looked up from her desk and smiled. "Yes? You look like you're a man with a mission."

I wasn't out of breath, but close to it. "Hoping to catch Deputy Wright or Agent Twiddy," I said, my words coming out in a rush.

"They're both out. Not sure where or when they'll be back." She tilted her head toward the room next door. "But FBI Agent Calvins is in there going over some records. Maybe he knows when Odell and Agent Twiddy will be back."

I nodded. "Thanks," I said.

The door to the office next door was opened a crack. I tapped lightly. I could see Agent Calvins sitting at the table, a number of papers spread out in front of him.

He motioned for me to come on in. I took the seat across from him. The financial papers he perused were what looked like bank statements or reports from banks. I remembered what he had said about following the money.

"I've got something interesting," I said. "I wanted to show it to you and Balls—Agent Twiddy—and Deputy

Wright."

A questioning expression on his face, but he didn't say anything.

I held my phone tightly. Turning it so he could see the picture of Eunice Cleave, I moved the image closer to him. He stared at it a moment and then at me.

"What's her name?" he said.

I told him and then how she had apparently befriended the two young women—Olga and Masha—who went missing, and were still missing and believed to be victims of human trafficking.

Lifting my chin and staring straight at Calvins, I said, "I believe Eunice Cleave and her brother Basil are involved."

FBI Agent Calvins didn't say anything. He only glanced at the picture again and then turned his gaze to me. He got that blank, noncommittal cop stare that I had seen many times before. It was a look lawmen tended to get when they knew something but didn't want you to know they knew. Holding back. Cards close to the chest.

He waited a long time without speaking. I waited too.

Then, slowly a warmth crept into his eyes; that warmth began to spread to his lips. He smiled at me. No longer was there that blank cop stare. He cleared his throat, the smile now genuine. "No wonder Ballsford calls you his lucky charm," he said. "You may have unlocked the last barrier to this case."

I waited, my eyes still on him. I was afraid to smile in return. I wanted to make sure he meant what he said.

Calvins removed his reading glasses, laid them carefully on the table, and rubbed one hand across his face and massaged his eyes.

"But stay away," he said. He said it softly, but with meaning.

"What?"

"Stay away from them," he said.

I tilted my head toward him. Questioning, but keeping

silent.

Calvins appeared to concentrate, staring down at the table, forming words in his mind. He wore a fresh dress shirt but at least didn't have on a tie today. Taking his time speaking, and obviously being careful how he phrased his thoughts, he said, "I realize that you've been involved in this from the beginning, and that you've been threatened with a phone call, and I acknowledge that Agent Twiddy and Chief Deputy Wright, and even the sheriff, trust you completely. But, and there's nothing disparaging implied by this statement: You're not authorized. You're not officially part of this investigation."

I couldn't keep quiet any longer. "I know that. Of course I do. But I wanted to pass on this information. This picture. Because I know—whether I'm official or not—that it has significance." My voice had risen. "And I would think that . . ."

He smiled at me and held both hands, palms up and forward, toward me. "Please," he said.

I shut up.

"Yes, the picture and that information does have significance. Great significance. And I'm stepping out of my official protocol in saying that it does. But . . ." And this time his voice trailed off as he appeared to struggle what to say next that would not jeopardize his so-called protocol.

Calvins puffed out a breath of air. He bore his eyes into mine. "There's a reason I want you to—that *we* will want you to—stay away from them, from Basil and Eunice Cleave. I'm not authorized to say much more than this: that they have my attention. Certainly now, and that's thanks to you. They will soon have *our* attention."

I was feeling a little bit better about this guy.

He waved a hand toward the pile of financial records he had been studying when I came in. "You remember I said something about following the money. That's what I've been doing, and with the help of the DHS, the Department of Homeland Security. They have some abilities—at least I'll call them 'abilities'—that we in the Bureau don't have, believe it or not."

Then he pointed to my phone, which I still held snuggly in hand. "And that picture you have and the intelligence surrounding it, put some real icing on the cake." He chuckled. "If you, as a writer, will permit me to talk in clichés."

I was beginning to feel even better about this guy.

He continued. "But we're not quite ready to move yet. And I don't want anything to interfere with our investigation as we get closer. I want you to stay away from them, not give them any reason to cover their tracks." He got a trace of a smile again. "In other words, I don't want you to intercourse it up." He actually chuckled. "How's that for polite writerly speech?"

Okay, I felt fine about this guy.

Then he asked if I could send him the picture of Eunice Cleave, which I could and did. Also, he wanted me to write a statement about how I got the picture and why it was taken, all of that background.

Mabel guided me to the office several of the deputies used from time to time and keyed up one of the computers that I could use to write my statement. In the meantime, Calvins went back to studying the hieroglyphics of the financial statements.

When I finished the statement and printed it out, including a copy for myself, I checked again with Calvins. He said he'd heard from Balls and Odell. They were over on the mainland trying to rundown more on the death of Micki Mitchell, whose body had been dumped along the highway. A couple of promising leads they followed hadn't panned out. They were checking into something else. Calvins said he would wait for them. He said he didn't tell them yet about the picture.

The afternoon was wearing on . . . and me along with it.

I told Calvins I was leaving. He nodded. "Thanks," he said, and went back to his financials, using a small calculator. He made notes on a yellow legal pad.

Speaking to Mabel, I thanked her for use of the computer. She seemed tired as she nursed a cup of hot tea and nibbled on something. "Want an oatmeal cracker?" she asked, pushing a small plate of them toward me. I took one. I could use it.

Leaving the courthouse, I walked around to my car on Sir Walter Raleigh Street. I thought about going into Downtown Books and speaking to Jamie. But I felt a bit drained and decided to drive on home.

On the way back to Kill Devil Hills, I played over in my mind what FBI Agent Larry Calvins had said to me about staying away from Eunice and Basil Cleave. Okay, I'd stay away. But that didn't mean I couldn't do a little checking.

And I knew how I would try to do that.

Chapter Twenty-Six

When I got home and went upstairs, I first checked on Janey, spoke to her, then picked up my narrow reporter's notepad from my desk. I stepped over the neck of the bass fiddle and went to the phone. No messages on the machine. I sat there a moment and I flipped through the pages of my notepad until I found the telephone number for Barbara and Dwight Reid, the first couple I talked with about drowning victim Marisa.

Well, they're neighbors of the Cleaves and it wouldn't hurt to contact Barbara and Dwight, sort of check in with them. Let it develop from there.

I punched in their telephone number. Barbara Reid answered. I identified myself and inquired how they were doing. She said they were doing about as well as could be expected.

"I hope you don't mind my call," I said, "but I wanted to let you know that I've not really learned anything about what party Marisa might have been going to that night." I paused a moment. "And I was double-checking with you to see if anything had occurred to you or your husband that might shed some light on it."

I knew that was pretty feeble. But she appeared to take it as perfectly normal.

"Not a thing," she said, "and we've thought about it a lot, and talked about it. Then with the stories I'm reading in the paper about everything else that is going on, we've just wondered . . . well, we've wondered that maybe . . ." She made a clucking sound, fishing for words. ". . . well, I guess we've wondered if maybe you don't think there's a connection between Marisa and these other things that are going on. The missing girls and then those killings." That was followed by a short laugh. "After all, you are a crime writer."

I tried to sound casual. "I'll admit I have a tendency to poke my nose into things—especially things that puzzle me. And I guess this one does. As to whether there's any connection, I'm sure the investigators are looking into all possibilities."

Then I got around to my real reason for calling. "I thought I'd check back with folks Marisa worked for and speak to them again. I assume maybe your neighbors—the Cleaves—have gone back to Maine?" I knew damn well they hadn't.

"Oh, no," Barbara said. "They're right here. In fact, they act like they may be getting ready to go on a trip in their boat." She paused, and then another one of those self-conscious short laughs. "I don't want to sound like the nosy neighbor, but they have had a couple of young men over there working on the boat. Looks like they're, you know, getting set to do more than just cruise out into the sound."

"That's certainly a nice boat," I said. "Big enough to take offshore."

"Oh, yes, they've taken it out in the ocean a number of times, I think."

I knew I was taking a chance on saying it, but I did anyway: "Be a nice boat for a party."

She was quiet a moment. With hesitancy in her voice, she said softly, "Yes . . . yes it would." Then one more of those short, nervous laughs. "You don't suppose . . . I mean, do you think . . ." She left it all unsaid.

"Oh, Mrs. Reid, I'm not supposing anything. Just commenting on what a nice boat it is." I had to extricate myself from this conversation, but I did want to plant a thought in her mind, and I think I did. "Since they're busy with workmen over there on the boat, I won't call them today."

"Yes . . ." she said, as if she were thinking of something else.

"A pleasure chatting with you, Mrs. Reid. If you do think of anything concerning Marisa—or anything that might be related—please give me a call. You've still got my card."

"Oh, yes. I've got your card right here."

I had the sense she wanted to stay on the phone longer, but I ended the conversation and we disconnected.

If I did my job, Barbara Reid was probably thinking about her neighbors right this minute, and I'd bet she would be watching them more closely.

After five, I called Elly at home. She said they hadn't been home long but that all went well at the pediatrician's and that Martin was all set to start preschool in now a little more than a week. "He was a brave little gentleman in the doctor's office," she said, and she said it loud enough that I know Martin was nearby and listening.

"Tomorrow night?" I said. "A regular Saturday night date? Heck, go to dinner, maybe even a movie. There's no limit to what we can do."

She laughed at my exaggerated exuberance. Her laughter is a musical sound, and I love it. "Sounds good," she said. Then she got more serious. "Anything exciting happen this afternoon?"

"I had a talk with FBI Agent Calvins. Seems like a nice guy."

"Uh-huh. Did you solve the case for him?"

"Well, I wanted to make sure he was doing his job."

"You can fill me in tomorrow. I've got a feeling something is up with you. Any time you get so . . . so upbeat, there's something percolating in that mind of yours."

"My mind just bubbles away when I talk with you."

"Yeah, sure," she said. "Get to work. Behave yourself, and I'll talk with you later."

We ended our conversation with me still smiling. I like her. Well, it's more than *like*, but that has to be a big part of it too.

I did get busy and spend close to an hour working on the final edits of that piece I was writing for Rose. Then I realized I should eat something. Soup and a grilled cheese sandwich, some fruit. That'd be fine.

Stepping out on the deck after I ate, I breathed in the evening air. I always believed I could smell the ocean at times like this. Light wind, the stars becoming visible. Beautiful night.

Later that night, after checking the news and weather reports on television, I partially covered Janey's cage and headed to bed. As usual, lying in bed I read several pages of the latest novel I was into—A Jack Reacher story by Lee Child.

At the time, as I relaxed and began to get sleepy, the investigation seemed a long way off.

That peaceful feeling, though, ended fairly early Saturday morning when Barbara Reid called.

I was having a cup of coffee out on the deck, enjoying another bright and sunny day, when the phone rang. I checked caller ID before I answered.

"Mr. Weaver? This is Barbara Reid. I hope I'm not calling too early."

"Not at all," I said. "How are you?"

"You said to call you if I thought of anything else, or something like that."

"Yes, that's good of you." I waited.

"Now, I don't want to sound like the nosy neighbor. You know the type that's always peeking out the window to see what the neighbors are doing. But I thought—and maybe I'm wrong to call—but I thought what I saw a while ago was very interesting and I thought it'd be best if I called you . . ."

I interrupted her to get her moving with it. I wanted to hear. "You did right to call, Mrs. Reid. What did you see?"

"What I saw was the Cleaves's car, that big dark-colored one. I never know the make. They're so much alike nowadays. Well, their car pulled up at their driveway and it wasn't Mr. Cleave driving but that man he has working for him on the boat, and there was another young man with him, and they got out and opened the back doors and two women—young ones—got out. Well, the two men actually helped the girls get out because the girls stumbled around a bit, like maybe—and I hate to say this—like maybe they were drunk or something."

"Yes, please go on, Mrs. Reid. That's most interesting." And it was indeed.

"Then the four of them went to the boat. The men had to practically push the girls onboard. And maybe they were, you know, pushing them, like maybe the girls hesitated."

I gripped the phone tightly. My mind was racing.

"Then they all got on the boat and the man who does the work on it, waved to someone standing on the back deck. I couldn't see who it was, but I guess it was either Mr. Cleave or his sister Eunice. The engine on the boat started up and there was a cloud of exhaust for a minute, and the boat pulled away from the dock, you know after they'd untied the ropes and everything."

My breathing was coming faster. I thought about calling Balls or trying to figure out how to track the boat, where it was going.

She continued, "But you said to call if . . . and I thought that was awfully strange this morning. I mean those two girls and all, and the way they sort of stumbled and were unsteady and then maybe pushed onto the boat. Like maybe even forced onto the boat."

"You did the right thing, Mrs. Reid. Thank you so very, very much." I wanted to get off the phone. "We'll certainly check into this."

"Well, I don't want you to think . . ."

"You did the right thing, as I said. Let me get busy checking something out. Thank you again. Goodbye."

She may have been trying to say something else, but I effectively cut her off.

Immediately I called Balls. The call went right to voice mail. I left him a rather cryptic message and asked him to call. Then I tried Odell at the sheriff's office. No luck there. Saturday morning. I hesitated only a moment before calling Odell's cell phone, get him at home probably.

He answered and I hurriedly told him what I knew and what Barbara Reid had related to me.

"We need to be able to track that boat," he said. "And I will alert Agent Calvins. I know he was considering that maybe they . . ."

"Yes, he told me to stay away from them."

"You did. Someone tipped you off. Half of our solid leads come as tips, you know that." There was silence from Odell. I could tell he wasn't through with what he had been saying. "And once again, Weav, you've come through with some really important information."

"Thanks, Odell." Then I said, "The name of the boat is the *Fantasy II.* It's probably a thirty-five footer. Flying bridge. A good size cabin below I'm sure."

"I'll see what we can do at this end. Maybe one of our deputies can take a ride in his boat, sort of surveillance." He paused a moment. "And I've got a contact down at the Oregon Inlet marina. He can let me know if the *Fantasy II* comes there, going out to sea."

We talked hurriedly for another few seconds. We disconnected.

Then a thought flashed in my mind. A way to track the *Fantasy II.*

By airplane.

I called Samantha Inez Davis, hoping I could catch her and that we could go flying.

Chapter Twenty-Seven

One of Sam's young pilots at her flying service answered the phone.

"Jimmy, this is Harrison Weaver. Is Sam there? I need to speak to her right away."

"I'm sorry Mr. Weaver, but she's not avail—Hold on a sec. She just came in."

Sam picked up.

My words came out in a rush. "This is Weav and we need to track a boat that's going out and—"

"Slow down." She said. "What are you talking about?"

I took a breath. "There's a boat we need to track. See what they are up to. They may be headed to Oregon Inlet and off shore. They left Kitty Hawk Bay a short while ago."

"Why do we need to track this boat?"

"Sam, they've got two young women on board, and I think well, you know what that's about."

"Uh-oh," she said. "You mean involved in what you've been looking into?"

"Yes."

"Where are you now? How soon can you get here?"

"I'm in Kill Devil Hills. I can be there in twenty or twenty-five minutes."

"I'll get the 172 gassed up." There was a smile in her voice. "And, Weav, this is going to cost you more than a hundred-dollar hamburger."

"I know, I know." She referred to the banter that pilots have been using for years: taking a student pilot to a nearby airport, practice a landing or two at a different airport, maybe grab a hamburger—which essentially costs a hundred bucks for the lesson and the hamburger.

"I'm on my way," I said. Grabbing my cell phone and wallet, I headed downstairs and hopped in my Outback. I drove out of my cul-de-sac and then onto the Bypass a lot faster than I like to, but today I'd take my chances. I probably offended some of the slower-moving drivers, especially those who were not familiar with the location of whatever it was they sought.

I was lucky with the traffic lights. Caught almost all of them on green and only had to squeeze through a yellow once. Offensive driving, with the emphasis on *offensive* as in bad.

But I made good time. Topping the bridge over Roanoke Island at sixty. Swung to the right going into Manteo and then was forced to slow down considerably. In twenty-two minutes, I was on the two-lane paved road leading to the airport.

I slammed into a parking space as close to the main terminal as possible and dashed into the building, taking the steps two at a time. Sam stood near the counter and as soon as I came in she said, "Let's go."

I matched her long stride as we scurried out to the Cessna. "I've already done the preflight check," she said. "And gassed up."

We got in, donned our headsets, and as we buckled up, she called, "Clear prop," and started the engine. Wasting no time, she taxied to the northeast end of the active runway. Light wind coming in from the south.

My cell phone chirped. It was Odell. I had to shout in the phone and move the headset away from the right ear so I could hear him say, "Can't get a deputy out in a boat for surveillance."

I told him we were about ready to take off and that cell phone communication would probably not be possible. I put the phone back in my pocket, readjusted the headset.

At the end of the taxiway, Sam revved the engine, checking the magnetos and testing the carburetor heat. Cycling the flight controls. She announced on the CTAF that we were taking off. We both scanned for any approaching aircraft. We were clear. She gave it full throttle and we rushed down the runway. She had us in the air in no time at all.

"Let's head to Pirate's Cove marina first," I said, "Check Albemarle Sound, and then fly south toward Oregon Inlet if we don't see the boat."

"Right," she said. There was sureness to her flying that I wished I could emulate. She climbed to slightly less than a thousand feet as we headed toward the Washington Baum Bridge and the marina. Over the bridge we banked sharply left and flew west and north up the sound. There were two small boats less than a quarter mile away. I shook my head at Sam; she kept us going up the sound. Nothing.

"We might as well head toward Oregon Inlet," I said.

Sam swung us around. She didn't drop any altitude on the turn, but we were low enough anyway to get a good view of any activity. I kept scanning the water below us. Looked over toward Wanchese. The usual fishing boats docked. One small johnboat came out into the sound, trailing a faint white wake.

Bodie Lighthouse was visible ahead and slightly to our left. No boat traffic that sparked interest.

We neared Oregon Inlet and the new, magnificent bridge over the inlet. A fairly large boat approached the bridge from the marina, heading toward the ocean.

"We'll take a look," Sam said, and she banked sharply again, the wing on my side of the aircraft pointing toward the water below. She brought us around so I could check out the boat. It was not the *Fantasy II* and a deck hand on board waved to us, and so did the captain, who stood tall at the wheel on the flying bridge. Then he went back quickly to steering his boat under the bridge to make the tricky passage out toward the ocean. The currents there and the shifting shoals can pose a problem.

"On out over the ocean a ways?" Sam said.

"Yes." I chewed on my lower lip, scanning back at the marina and then out to sea. "I didn't think they could have gotten this far from Kitty Hawk," I said. "But, maybe they could."

"More time has elapsed than you may realize since you called me," she said. "And if they had just left then, and they went fast, they could have cleared Oregon Inlet by now." She glanced over at me. "What makes you think they were coming this way, anyway?"

She had a point. "There were not that many places to go," I said, "unless they decided to go up the Intracoastal Waterway. And I can't believe they'd do that." I didn't say it, but I was thinking that if they wanted to traffick those two young women, they'd probably go offshore and either meet someone or take them farther south to unload them at another port.

"So, out to sea a ways?" Sam said again.

"Yes."

She held our altitude at eight hundred feet. We both scanned ahead and to the right and left. I saw a boat up to the north. I pointed toward it and she headed that way, dropping down to five hundred feet. As we got closer, I saw the twin outriggers deployed to its sides. A commercial fishing boat. While I wasn't familiar with all of the ins and outs of commercial fishing, I figured the outriggers were dragging a net. Shrimpers, I assumed.

"Nope," I said, and pointed south.

Sam banked and turned smoothly. Air currents bobbled us gently. Overall it was very smooth flying in that cloudless blue sky with the sun glistening off the water below.

I saw three porpoises skimming along close to the surface. One of them leaped into the air. A beautiful sight, and I wished we could have spent more time enjoying it.

We were out about five miles I estimated, when down to my right I saw a boat in the distance. I touched Sam's shoulder and pointed.

"Take a look?" she said.

I nodded. "Please."

Sam nosed the Cessna down to five hundred feet. Then even lower. About three hundred feet. She slowed as much as she could. I figured the stall warning horn might go off at any moment. Glad a pilot as good as Sam was flying. We were closer to the water than I would like to be with anyone other than Sam.

As we approached the boat I squinted hard at the stern. Bingo!

It was the *Fantasy II.*

"There it is," I said.

She nodded, concentrating on flying.

Three people were on the back deck and a single person was at the wheel in the flying bridge. Two of those on the back deck were women. One of them stood and began waving. She looked familiar, and then I realized it was Janika, the pretty girl who had served me at Claire's.

She wobbled a bit. I couldn't tell whether it was from movement of the boat or whether she was unsteady on her feet. The other woman waved too but didn't try to stand. I wasn't sure what their waves meant. They were either grinning at us or crying out to us.

Sam circled back around. The plane sank a bit—and so did my stomach. At three hundred feet I felt like we could reach out and touch the people on the boat.

The man at the wheel—and I was sure it was the same man I'd seen working on the engine at Cleave's house—appeared to be yelling something at the young man on the deck, who stood there staring up at us. Then the young man hurried to the women. He grabbed the arm of the one who was standing unsteadily on her feet and pushed her toward the door to the cabin and pointed. He rushed to the other woman, dragged her to her feet and pushed her up against the other one, who still stood in front of the cabin door. He opened the cabin door and shoved them both inside.

The man at the wheel was apparently still yelling instructions at the young man down on the deck.

We circled around for the third time. Sam busily kept us flying. She banked sharply toward my side. But then on the next circle she banked so that her wing tip pointed at the boat.

That's when things really got dicey.

The young man half stumbled to a hatch on the port side of the rear deck, reached in, and came out with a gun.

A short automatic weapon, like an Uzi.

He raised it toward us.

Chapter Twenty-Eight

He began firing. I could see the muzzle flashes but couldn't hear the reports.

But I heard bullets hitting the Cessna. Loud pings or thumps, depending on where the bullets hit.

Off in the distance to the south, a speedboat headed toward us. As soon as the gunfire started, though, the speedboat came to an abrupt halt, swung around, and began speeding in the opposite direction.

"Get out of here," I yelled into the headset.

There was another burst of gunfire.

She didn't say anything but shoved full power on and pulled back on the yoke at the same time and we zoomed up over the boat below. Gaining altitude fast.

But not fast enough. There were more bullet hits.

Sam made a noise, like sucking in air loudly. There was surprise and pain in her face—and fear, too. She gripped the yoke firmly, deep furrows between her eyebrows. She was shaking her head.

Then she looked down at her left side, just above her hip. She put her right hand on her side and it came away bloody, and then more blood began to ooze through her T-shirt and shorts.

"Oh, shit," she said.

I think I said the same thing.

She had turned the aircraft around, headed back toward shore.

"Call," she said. "Mayday." Her voice was strained.

I grabbed the mic hanging from the instrument panel. Turned the frequency to 121.5, pushed the talk button and shouted, "Mayday. Mayday. Mayday. This is Cessna four six three niner zero about six miles off Oregon Inlet."

I released the button to listen and within seconds Air Traffic Control came back with, "Cessna four six three niner zero. This is Cherry Point Marine Corps Air Station. Stay on this frequency. What is your emergency?"

"We've taken gunfire from a boat. The pilot is wounded. I'm a student and I'm flying back to Manteo."

"Do you need a heading to Manteo, and are you capable of landing?"

"I think I can land it. I've got to. But we'll need medical help. Yes, a heading would be good."

Sam, her voice weak, said, "Transponder." I fumbled to set it to the emergency code 7700, which would show bright on every radar within range.

ATC said, "We have you on radar. Ten miles southeast of Manteo. Fly heading three two zero and report Manteo in sight. Will arrange for an ambulance."

"Roger. Heading three two zero." It felt good to have some help. I brought it around to the heading, wings wobbling.

"The boat that fired on us is heading south. It's *Fantasy II*, a thirty-five footer with a flying bridge. Two males on board and two women shoved into the cabin, being abducted, we think."

"Copy that, Cessna two niner zero. We will alert the Coast Guard."

"Take the controls," Sam whispered weakly.

"Okay. Got 'em," I said, grabbing the passenger-side yoke with both hands.

Her head seemed to bob as if her neck could not support

it. "A towel." She said. "Behind my seat."

I twisted my left arm around trying to get the towel. Felt like I pulled something in my shoulder. Straining. My fingers touched the edge of the towel. Stretching as much as I could against the harness, I got hold of it and brought it out. It was a blue cotton hand towel that wasn't too clean. But I handed it to Sam and she used it to press against her side. There was more blood.

Her head drooped and I thought for a moment she had passed out. Then she said, "You have to take us back, Weav."

"It's okay. I've got it," I said. But I was terrified. Breath coming fast. Then I think ATC said, "Good luck Cessna two niner zero We will monitor until you're down safely"

We were going to need some luck. That was for damn sure.

I kept glancing over at Sam. She didn't look good. There was more blood. We were at five hundred feet. I eased in a bit more power, applied backpressure on the yoke and got us up to eight hundred feet, which I had learned was pattern altitude at Manteo. The Bodie Lighthouse was in the distance. I headed toward it. Once I got there, I knew I could find the airport.

Sam's head had sunk down again.

Land this damn thing? Oh, crap. I had to. She was in no condition.

"Sam," I said. "Hang on. Don't leave me. Stay with me, Sam."

She mumbled something.

I was sweating. With my right forearm and then my hand, I wiped at my face. My left hand was gripping the yoke rigidly, and I tried to relax it. Fly more smoothly.

I tried to remember everything Samantha had taught me.

She raised her head a moment, then stared at the growing flood of blood on her side and hip. Weakly she brushed the towel at the blood and then pressed it again against her side, and her head drooped again.

I stopped concentrating on her and looked straight ahead. Made sure I was still flying level and on heading. Wingtips even with the horizon. Holding eight hundred feet.

The village of Wanchese came into view down to my left at about ten o'clock.

Manteo and the airport should be in view in less than a minute.

Sam muttered something.

"I didn't understand, Sam."

She tried again. "You can land it."

I knew I would have to try my best. Couldn't let fear get in the way. I tried to take deep breaths, in through my nose, out through my mouth. It didn't really work. I wiped at my face again.

The airport came into view, like someone had painted a landscape with the trees at this end and the Croatan Sound at the other end.

I checked the windsock, saw it was going to be a slight crosswind, and pulled off some power, letting us descend. I was going to try to bring the plane straight in. I remembered to call ATC and they came back with, "We have you approaching the active at Manteo. All other traffic has been suspended. You are cleared to land runway two three."

I managed to say, "Roger, cleared for two three." Like I knew what I was doing.

The runway was drawing closer and I was still descending. A quick glance at Sam. She must have felt the plane slowing and sinking because she appeared to be trying to raise her head.

As she had told me, I picked out a spot on the runway where I wanted to touch down. Keep that spot steady in the windscreen.

Out of the corner of my vision, I saw two Dare County ambulances off to the side, a full-size fire truck and a smaller one, plus the county's medical evacuation helicopter, rotors turning. Two police cruisers were there. Several people stood near the vehicles watching my approach.

The touchdown spot I had picked out began to drop on my windscreen. Drop way too much.

Sam roused herself enough to say, "Too high, too high. Go around."

I had put in thirty degrees of flaps. When she told me to go around, I pulled back sharply on the yoke and retracted the flaps.

Uh-oh. The stall horn sounded really loud and the plane actually began to shudder. About to stall. Which would kill us both.

I lowered the nose and slammed in it full power. I was over the far end of the runway and the water of the sound was moving toward me fast. Very fast.

With backpressure on the yoke, I tried to get the nose up in time. I barely made it. I couldn't have been more than two hundred feet above the water when I began to climb steadily under full power.

I went back around, flying over the terminal and the parked vehicles at five hundred feet. About a quarter of a mile beyond the runway, I made a sharp right turn to the base leg, another right turn and I was lined up with the runway.

And now too low.

I saw the tall pines coming up fast in front of me. Sure as hell wanted to clear them.

I did, with a few yards to spare.

I was leaning forward, hard against my harness.

Powering down.

Only about a wing-length from the runway, and the damn plane wanted to keep on flying, floating. I cut back even more on the power and we dropped.

And bounced hard.

We came up off the ground, then bounced again. Another hard one. Then we were down and rolling.

I must have inadvertently pushed the left rudder pedal

because the aircraft skewed sharply to the left. It felt like I might be ripping the rubber off the tires. But I applied right rudder and it straightened out.

I had the plane more or less under control now and I began a fast taxi toward the emergency vehicles. But they were coming toward me as I slowed. Powering down almost completely, I applied both toe brakes and brought the plane to a stop. Killed the engine. Felt immense relief. Pried my left hand off the yoke.

Both ambulances sped up and slammed to halts close by. The EMTs bounded out and rushed toward us.

Chapter Twenty-Nine

I looked over at Sam. There was no color in her face. She was trying to move her head. "We made it, Sam. We made it."

As the EMTs rushed up, pushing a gurney between them, I unbuckled my harness and reached over and released Sam's. My hand came away bloody. She moaned and tried to say something. Her eyes fluttered open and shut.

They came around to the pilot's side and jerked open the door. I started getting out. Another tech stood by to help me. "I'm okay," I said, but he still put a hand on my elbow and then on my shoulder as I eased out. I was shaky. My legs felt weak and I was trembling. Deep breaths. The tech concentrated on my face. "I'm okay," I said again.

Sam groaned as they eased her out and onto the gurney. She rolled her head from side to side. Her face was contorted with pain. Three EMTs began working on her immediately. One of them cut away the waistband of her shorts and packed a bandage on the wound. Another one took her vital signs and the third fitted her with oxygen. They shared information with each other. Blood pressure was low and the woman who took the vitals began an IV attachment to the back of her right hand. They tried to staunch the flow of blood and one said something about a clotting medicine.

I came around to her, trying not to get in the way of the

EMTs, and shouted over the roar of the helicopter's engine, "You're going to be all right, Sam. You're going to make it." I'm not sure she heard me.

One of the EMTs jostled me a bit and I stepped back and watched them cover her with a blanket and race the gurney over to the waiting helicopter.

"Where?" I called to one of the EMTs.

"Norfolk," he said. "The acute trauma center."

The helicopter's rotors whirled. The side door was open and they loaded Sam aboard and two of the EMTs jumped in behind her.

The chopper lifted off and headed north fast.

Going back toward the Cessna, I saw Jimmy, one of Sam's pilots, staring in the pilot's door. He saw all the blood and the color leeched from his face. He shook his head. "We'll push it over to the line and tie it down," he said. Two more of Sam's crew came up and helped.

I walked toward the terminal. My legs still felt funny, like they didn't quite want to do right.

Deputy Dorsey came toward me, a worry of concern on his face, which was shiny with perspiration. I stopped so he could talk to me. He started to speak, but I said, "Let's go on in." I wanted water and I wanted to sit down.

"Sure," he said.

The medical tech walked with us to the terminal and then he left us and went back to one of the ambulances.

Inside the terminal, the husky man behind the counter leaned forward. "Sam gonna be all right?"

"I think so," I said. "She sure better be."

The man nodded, a worried look on his face.

Then he said, "I saw you land."

"It was pretty bad," I said.

"Hey, you know what they say. If you can walk away from a landing, it's a good landing."

I plopped down on the leatherette sofa. Looking up at Deputy Dorsey, I said, "Water?"

"I'll get some." He came back in a moment with a cold bottle. He had loosened the cap.

I drank at least a third of it without stopping.

Dorsey sat on the edge of the sofa, turned slightly toward me.

I said, "Balls—SBI Agent Twiddy—and Odell. Where are they?"

Dorsey wiped at his face with the palm of one hand and then ran the hand over his close-cropped reddish hair. A trace of a triumphant smile: "They've gone, along with that FBI guy, to apprehend Basil Cleave and his sister Eunice." He sat straighter. "They're involved."

"I know," I said.

"And that's not all. The Coast Guard and DHS intercepted that boat. Got the two guys and freed the women." He swelled his chest out. "Jail's gonna be crowded tonight."

By Tuesday, medical reports were that Sam was recovering nicely and could have visitors. The bullet that hit her had torn through the lower part of the pilot door before striking her, tearing up a good chunk of her side but not breaking anything. The slug was apparently ragged when it hit her, and slowed by the door. It was a messy wound and she lost a whole lot of blood.

The two men from the boat were still in custody. The two young women were treated at the hospital—they had been heavily drugged. But they recovered and planned to go back to work in a few days. Before they left the Outer Banks Hospital, I managed to have a moment to speak with Janika. I didn't know the other woman. Janika was embarrassed to talk, but after a few minutes she relaxed and spoke more openly. She said something, her voice soft and sad, that stuck with me, something I'd always remember. She said, "All any of us wanted was summer at the beach, a good dream, and we didn't know it would be so . . . so deadly."

The Cleaves had been released on a hefty bond but weren't going anywhere. Their passports confiscated. They had tried to claim that their boat had been stolen. The FBI wasn't buying that and neither were the investigators from the Department of Homeland Security.

Balls is convinced they'll do time. Too much evidence built up earlier by the FBI and DHS that they were the local heads of a widespread human trafficking scheme. Some of the girls had been sold as sex slaves to a cartel in Columbia. I thought about the boat that had been racing toward the *Fantasy II* until the shooting started. That was probably some of the traffickers from Columbia.

Elly got off from work Tuesday to go with me up to the Norfolk hospital to visit Sam. Before we left Manteo, Elly insisted we stop and get flowers to take. I hadn't thought about that and I was glad she did.

At the hospital, we checked about the room. The woman behind the desk tried to insist that visiting hours didn't start for two hours. But we pleaded with her and mentioned how far we had driven to pay a visit and the woman relented.

"Say you're relatives, if anyone asks," she said.

The usual antiseptic smells followed us down the corridors. It was relatively quiet and our shoes made a slight squeaking on the polished floor.

Sam's room door was partially open. A nurse was leaving. Sam was propped up just a bit in the bed. An IV was attached to the back of her right hand. A bottle of fluid was suspended from a hook on a stand beside her bed. A monitor blinked with information. But she looked better than I thought she would. Her hair was brushed back from her face, which was still rather pale. Maybe it was partly the light.

Elly added our flowers to several vases that were already there. Sam said, "Thank you. They're pretty." Her voice was soft but not real weak.

She smiled and I took her hand.

We visited for only about ten minutes or so.

As we prepared to leave, Sam managed another smile at me.

Then, sounding more like her old self, she said, "We've really got to work on your landings."